"I'm in! *I*  They want me!" place now. Brett, ~~Palm Canyon~~, everything. It was all mine. I was a newcomer and it was all mine. I had no idea I would feel this way. The idea of becoming a member of Chi Kappa had been so remote that it had seemed beyond the perimeters of my life. If the sorority hadn't invited me to become a member, I would have said "Who cares?" and I would have meant it. But the reality of being asked to join opened up all my dreams of really belonging in Palm Canyon. Part of that sorority table in the cafeteria would truly be mine for the remainder of my high school career. Even if I sat alone there from time to time, I wouldn't care. Because everyone would know I belonged.

ALSO AVAILABLE IN LAUREL-LEAF BOOKS:

SORORITY SISTERS #1

For Members Only

Marjorie Sharmat

Published by
Dell Publishing Co., Inc.
1 Dag Hammarskjold Plaza
New York, New York 10017

Laurel-Leaf Library ® TM 766734, Dell Publishing Co., Inc.

ISBN: 0-440-92654-8

RL: 5.5

Printed in the United States of America

June 1986

10 9 8 7 6 5 4 3 2 1

WFH

*For Andrew
with love and thanks
for your absolutely Blitzful ideas*

1

I needed a plan. I had moved to Palm Canyon, Arizona, and the city wasn't ready for me. Brett Fox, whom I met the first day of school and fell in love with the first day of school, wasn't ready for me. The girls I wanted to be friends with weren't ready for me. If you want my opinion, Palm Canyon was an ill-prepared city.

My parents moved themselves and me to the sunny Southwest because they were tired of the East and tired of snow, but mainly because they had a lot of money and could afford to do things that might turn out to be extremely foolish. But they loved it here right away. They made friends and bought a beautiful home, and my father even got a job the very first week. Palm Canyon was ready for *them*.

I don't have my parents' flair. I'm insecure. At the beginning of the summer I turned sixteen. I was shy up until then. But now I'm old enough for the more sophisticated label of *insecure*. Not that anybody calls me that, except me. A look in the mirror tells me I'm pretty, but I don't connect to that adjective—even when people say it.

My parents may have flair, but their timing
could be improved. We moved here just before the school year began. If we had moved a
little sooner, I might have picked up a friend
or two before school started. I might have
dumped my label.

I walked to school that first day by myself,
of course. It was warm, but I knew that by the
middle of the day it would be hot. Around
now back east there would be a nip in the air
and fall leaves and all the other things that are
routinely associated with fall. No legitimate
autumn season could be without them. So autumn in the Southwest must be illegitimate or
phony or something. And Palm Canyon High
School doesn't look like a legitimate high
school either. Palm trees, saguaro cactus
around the buildings, mountains rising in the
background. It looks like a vacation resort.
Maybe the kids who grew up here think this is
just the way a high school is supposed to look.

Nobody, but nobody, spoke to me during
my first classes. At lunchtime I sat alone with
my tray of food at a table in the cafeteria. I
was thinking about my old high school. If
there is anything high school teaches you beyond the stuff you learn in books, it's the caste
system. There's the royalty, the peasants, and
all the kids in between. Some of them try to
ignore the whole business, but most of them

frantically rush to elevate themselves to the next rung. I, Kim Adler, new girl in town, didn't even have a rung. When you're new, sometimes you're wildly popular because you're a novelty. Or . . . you're wildly ignored because you're a nonentity.

I was sitting in the cafeteria, wildly ignored, when a girl put her food tray next to mine on the table. It looked like she had doubles of everything. Steakettes, Tater Tots, string beans, biscuits, and peach crisp, served with a half pint of milk, was the meal of the day.

"Hi," she said. "I'm Elissa Hanes. You're new in school?"

I nodded.

Elissa sat down beside me. She was kind of fat. Maybe not fat enough to bring out the cruelty in kids, but probably fat enough to disqualify her from being really *in* in Palm Canyon High. Maybe she was looking for a friend the way I was looking for a friend. I was thin the way Elissa was fat. It wasn't the kind of thin that's sometimes called slim or slender. Just thin.

"Please don't comment on what I'm eating," she said as she started to eat. "The kids look at my food, then back at me, then back at my food. Tomorrow I'm going on a diet. What's you name?"

"Kim Adler. I moved here from New York."

"I'm a native. Want the tour?"

"What tour?"

"For openers, the cafeteria tour. Who's sitting where, who you should fawn over if you happen to be a fawner, which I'm not, who's dangerous, who's . . ."

"Who's that bunch over there?" I asked. "In the corner."

"You mean Buckingham Palace? That's the cafeteria residence of Chi Kappa Sorority."

"This school has a sorority?"

"Not officially. In fact, the administration doesn't approve of it. Chi Kappa was started nine or ten years ago when a couple of girls decided that all the school clubs were too blah. These two girls got together and slowly added eight more. The sorority did pretty much as it pleased for a few months until the school administration got wind of it and put on the pressure. The sorority disbanded for a little while but then it started up again and now it's going stronger than ever. You can always find some of the members eating together over at that table. The one on the end is Tracy McVane. She's editor of the high school newspaper. On her right is Carrie Reis, a cheerleader. The bright blonde is Rona Dunne. She practically runs the school just on her own popularity. There's ten members in all. No more. No less. Ten shiny, exclusive slots to be filled from the ranks of the girls of Palm Canyon High."

"Sounds awful."

"Well, it's cliché popularity, you know. A cheerleader, a newspaper editor, a beautiful blonde, and that's the kind of popularity that gives the high school years their deservedly rotten reputation."

"It's not fair for a few kids to have the power."

"High school fair? You expect a lot, Kim. Shall we go on to another table? We have democratic tables, also. We have kids who toil and sweat and pass four years in colorless obscurity. Some of them will become famous out there in the real world one day, but not today. So, who else can I tell you about? Want an introduction to anybody?"

"Uh . . ."

"Male or female. I'm not shy."

"I am. I mean I'm not shy anymore because I'm sixteen and—well, forget it. It's too hard to explain."

"You can accomplish with me what it might take you weeks on your own to do."

I wondered if Elissa had some kind of motive or was just being nice or what.

"Pick a person," she insisted.

Brett Fox walked into the cafeteria on cue. I didn't know his name then. I only knew his impact. On me. He was a *presence*. Big, rugged, brown-haired, brown-eyed. He came with his own magnetic field. I was drawn to him.

I pointed to him. "Him," I said. "I want to meet him."

How could I have said that? But I really did!

I suddenly pictured myself in this school for two full years, eyeing this guy, never getting a chance to meet him, our paths never colliding. Admiring Someone Hopelessly from Afar is one of the burdens borne by insecure people. Insecure people who don't have a helpful friend like Elissa.

"I don't know him," she said.

"You didn't know me, but that didn't stop you."

I think that was a half compliment, half insult. I didn't intend it as an insult. An incentive was what I had in mind.

"You're a girl," she said.

I knew she was going to say that.

"Okay, forget it. I'll meet him on my own sometime."

"No, I think he's new in school. We have to do it before he's discovered and the line forms."

Elissa raised a plump arm. She was wearing a long-sleeved dress and the sleeves were loose. When she raised her arm, the sleeve fell back. Her arms seemed to be the heaviest part of her. Elissa was beckoning to Brett with her index finger. I was embarrassed. Her finger was saying "Come here, you" to a stranger.

I was the girl who had needed a plan. And now one was forming. It was simple. Take advantage of every opportunity that comes your way. Go for it. Don't shrink back. Passivity can make you invisible.

If only Brett hadn't looked so astonished! But who could blame him. A plump unknown arm and index finger reacting with great animation to your presence. It's enough to throw anyone off. Still, he started to walk toward us.

"Lower your arm, Elissa," I said. "It did a good job."

"I know how to pick people up," she said. "If I weren't such a scholar and if I weren't overweight, I could easily make it as a hooker."

Brett Fox walked toward us. He was carrying some books under one arm. He was very, very tall. Finally he was standing across the table, facing us.

"I'm Elissa Hanes," Elissa said. "And your name is . . . ?"

"Brett Fox." He smiled. At me. It was the smile of a very tall person. That's hard to explain. It just was. "Your name?" he asked me.

"I was coming to that," Elissa said. "She's Kim Adler and she's a friend of mine."

I knew that Elissa was bright enough to know that we couldn't possibly be friends by virtue of time spent together or confidences exchanged. But feelings counted the most, and somehow we both had the feeling of friendship. It wasn't because she was too fat and I was too thin and we were both equally distanced from perfection. I *liked* Elissa and I knew she liked me.

"Hi," I said to Brett. "Nice to meet you."

He answered, "Nice to meet you." He emphasized *you,* but in an exchange like this, the second person is always stuck with emphasizing the word *you.* Otherwise the conversation can sound like a broken record.

"Kim's new in town," Elissa said. "You must be too. I don't recall ever having seen you."

"I've just moved here from New York," he said.

"So have I!" I exclaimed, hoping that this was the most important and significant coincidence ever to happen in the life of Brett Fox. This was my landmark coincidence, I was sure of it. This was fate, the Real Meaning behind my moving to Palm Canyon.

"Oh?" he said as if I had just given him last week's weather report.

My excited reaction must have sounded

like Elissa's beckoning arm had looked. She and I were a couple of winners.

"Everybody's from New York," said Elissa. "Except the people from Minnesota. Why Minnesota? Beats me. Oh, excuse me, I get caught up in monologues. Is that the same as liking to hear yourself talk?"

Brett smiled and I smiled. Then he said, "Mind if I join you?" and he sat down while he said it.

"You don't have any food," said Elissa.

"In a minute," he said. He looked at me. "What part of New York are you from? New York, New York, or somewhere else in the state?"

"New York, New York," I said. I was beginning to feel happy. It was a simple, warm feeling. It had begun slowly when Elissa joined me, but now excitement seemed to be at its core.

I didn't want to just stare at Brett. My gaze kind of drifted beyond him. Suddenly I realized that someone was staring at me. At us. A girl with red hair and ambitious eyes was looking at Brett and me as if she had paid good money, cold cash, for the chance, and she was going to get her money's worth. I found out later that her name was Crystal Jameson and she, like me, was a girl with plans.

2

Elissa reminded Brett again that he didn't have any food. She offered him half of her lunch, which would have left her with one full lunch. But he excused himself to go buy something. He said he'd be right back.

"Anyone else you'd like to meet?" Elissa asked matter-of-factly as she dug into her string beans.

"Do you do this all the time?" I asked. "Introduce people?"

Elissa wolfed down a biscuit. "No. Very selectively. I'm not crazy about a number of kids in this school. But you I like."

"Why?"

"You're a good kid, I can tell."

Elissa was concentrating on her food. I still wondered why she had zeroed in on me so fast, and why she was so generous with what might be called her introductory offers. Sometimes kids try to buy friendship without being aware of it. But Elissa was a hip person. Did she want something from me? Was she my friend, but with strings attached?

She looked up from her food. "I just introduced you to the man of your dreams, didn't I?"

I looked down at my food. My lunch was the same as hers, except half as much. "It's too soon to know anything as important as that."

"No, it isn't," she said.

I couldn't admit that I thought I was in love. But I certainly could admit that I owed her something. "Thanks for what you did," I said. "If I can ever introduce you to anybody. I mean, later because I don't know anybody yet. Actually I was trying to figure out some sort of master plan for getting this city to acknowledge me."

"Crystal Jameson's acknowledging you. She's watching you."

"Crystal Jameson?"

"The redhead over there. The one who just followed Brett to the cafeteria line. She's been looking you over. Or you and Brett. She moved here last winter, in the middle of the school year, and she's been busy trying to establish herself ever since."

"How do you do that? Establish yourself?"

Elissa gave me a wary look. "Maybe you don't want to. Sometimes it's better to be out than in."

"You can't mean that."

Elissa ran her fingers through her short brown hair. She looked serious, suddenly, and her face looked older, like her face of the future, a preview of Elissa at thirty-five. Just as suddenly her youth was restored. She grinned. "Eat your string beans, kid."

But I knew I wouldn't forget that future face.

Brett came back with a full tray, and he sat down across the table from us again. He started to eat and he started to talk. Some people can't do both at the same time gracefully. He could.

"Tell me all about your past," he said to me. "Your wicked life back east."

"Tell me too," Elissa said. "But only if it's wicked."

Brett laughed. He had strong, good teeth that looked as if they had developed on high-quality red meat, fresh fruits and vegetables, and pure white top-grade milk. Some guys have fast-food teeth.

For the first time, I noticed what he was wearing. A brown and white striped shirt with an open collar and short sleeves. I don't know if he noticed what I was wearing. I have long hair and I often push it behind my ears. Mostly I like it around my face. My father calls my hair golden. He says that anybody can be a blonde, but golden is something different. Golden hair is the stuff of fairy-tale heroines. I'm really in no danger of being mistaken for a fairy-tale heroine. I'm in no danger of being irresistible or of having guys drop dead at my feet. Still, I'm not going to sell myself short. Just before I left New York, Sidney Megovitch asked me to marry him. He's thirteen, but he's much sexier than his name. Smart too. He said he knew we'd have to wait several years. Also he knew there was an age difference in the wrong categories. I, the girl, was older. In New York he seemed like a thirteen-year-old pest. But now out here, with time and space between us, he had developed into a fantastic compliment. Imagine, getting a marriage proposal at age sixteen, and barely sixteen at that. Brett Fox, I hope you appreciate me. Maybe you've got something good here.

I sort of tossed my fairy-tale hair. It's an affectation, the only one I'm aware that I have. "My past isn't wicked," I said finally. "So tell me about yourself. How come you moved to Palm Canyon?"

"My mother got transferred. Her company offered her a promotion to move out here. She's got a good job."

"And your father?" Elissa asked.

"He's looking for a good job." Brett smiled.

"I don't believe this," Elissa said.

"That my father's looking for a good job and my mother has one?" Brett kept smiling.

"That I believe," said Elissa. "It's Crystal Jameson. She went over to the sorority table and she just plain sat down without being asked. One, two, three like that."

"What's the sorority table?" Brett turned around to look.

"The members of Chi Kappa Sorority sit at that table over there, as if it's reserved for them. They stick together, scheme together, and rule the school together."

"What if somebody else sits there first?" Brett asked.

"They learn not to." Elissa's expression turned fiendish. "Crystal Jameson hasn't learned," she said. "Or maybe she has, and she's trying to worm her way in. Sometimes the sorority girls invite an outsider to sit down, but Crystal just took her tray and *sat*. She's trying to get asked in, I know it. Two members graduated last year, leaving two vacancies, you might say. Crystal's trying to fill one of them."

Brett was sizing up the table. "Is she the pretty redhaired girl?" he asked.

That's the way it is. The girl at a distance gets the compliment. The girl who doesn't hear the compliment or know that it's been given.

"Beauty is in the eye of the beholder," Elissa said. It made me feel worse.

"You coining phrases again, Elissa?" A guy had come over and was standing beside Brett.

His voice was mocking. "I'm floored by your originality."

"I'll revive you," Elissa answered in a sarcastic voice, and I knew that they were used to kidding each other. But she was looking up at him with an expression that was pure Sidney Megovitch in love. Did this guy know it? Or did he just think of her as a pal? It seemed that way. Elissa would be shocked if she knew that I, the newcomer, already had figured out what she probably hoped was her big secret.

The guy sat down. "Kim, Brett, this is Eric . . . oh, dear, Eric, I forgot your last name."

She *really* liked him! She was keeping the game going.

Eric wasn't. "I'm Eric Day," he said to Brett and me. "You two are new, aren't you?"

"Does everybody notice the newcomers around here?" I asked.

"We're a small school as high schools go," said Eric. "The giant high school is on the other side of town. Newcomers might slip in unnoticed there. What's the matter? Don't you like the attention?"

"I wasn't getting any until I sat down here," I said before I could stop myself.

"And Elissa sat down beside you, right?" Eric said.

"How did you know? Have you been watching us?"

"No."

Then how *did* he know? I glanced sideways at Elissa, but she had clammed up. That is, she had stopped talking. But she was eating furiously. Hunger, embarrassment, habit, primal urge . . . whatever was driving her, she was cleaning up her tray fast.

Eric was suddenly tight-lipped too. Everything about him was tight, compact. Tightly curled hair, small, almost girlish features, a lean trim build.

But why the silence? What was the mystery? Brett was looking at me sympathetically. But not for long. He stood up and said, "I'd better get a head start to my next class. I'm still finding my way around this place. I'll be seeing you guys."

Brett took his tray away, and then came back for his books. "I should have put these in my locker," he said. "Wherever it is." Then he said to me, "I'd still like to talk New York with you sometime."

He left, walking tall, you might say, and walking confident too. Soon all the girls would be ogling him in the hallways and classrooms.

Elissa finished her meal. Eric didn't have a tray. He wasn't eating.

"Best steakettes I've ever had," Elissa said cheerfully.

They must have been mind-altering

steakettes, too, because Elissa's mood had shifted back to lively.

Eric's face loosened. All was well again.

But I felt uncomfortable. I looked over at the sorority table. I wondered if any of those girls would ever walk up to me the way Elissa had. Or had Elissa, an outsider, already established me as an outsider too? Right now the only tangible thing I had was the instant friendship of Elissa Hanes. Did she pick up every newcomer in town?

Being new is a lot like being stupid. In both cases, there are lots of things you don't know.

3

My parents had sent me off to school that day with specific instructions. My father's: "Knock 'em dead." My mother's: "Be sure to remove any price tags on your new clothes."

I knew my mother was going to grill me like crazy when I got home. Did you make any friends? How are your teachers? Did anyone remark about your hair? My mother was proud of my hair.

But when I got home from school that afternoon, Mom was sitting on the patio by the pool with two other women. She introduced them as Epsy Tass and Joanna McVane. They both had short blond hair, slight tans, and slender limbs, and they looked like they belonged to charge accounts at posh stores. No way could these women be poor. They were sitting beside a swimming pool that didn't belong to them, and in front of elaborate desert plantings that didn't belong to them, and an expensive panoramic mountain view that didn't belong to them, and yet if you took all these things away, the two women would still look like Ladies of the Charge Account. My mother is short, and she has brown hair and freckles, and her aura is army and navy surplus. Except when she's on the golf course, where she has a pro look, but not the talent.

I told the two ladies I was happy to meet them.

They were looking me over, evaluating my worth.

"I met Epsy and Joanna at the golf course," my mother explained. "They each have daughters at Palm Canyon High. One of them is a junior like you."

"My daughter is Tracy McVane," Joanna McVane said. "If you don't know her already, I'm sure you will. She's editor of the school newspaper. A junior, and editor of the paper. We're very proud of her."

I remembered that Tracy McVane was one of the sorority girls. My mother was sitting with a sorority mother. What difference did that make except that it seemed to be such a big deal to sit with the sorority girls. Was there a mothers' table set up somewhere in Palm Canyon?

"You really should meet Tracy soon," Joanna McVane went on. "I'm sure the two of you would hit it off."

On the basis of my having said approximately five words, trite words at that, Joanna McVane was sure that her daughter and I would hit it off. This was not love at first sight, but love at first appraisal. I was the daughter of a kidney-shaped swimming pool, a ten-thousand-dollar landscaping job, an acre lot, and 3,400 square feet of living space in what was known as the fashionable foothills. We lived slightly above our means, but got away with it through the years. We have a bunch of rich relatives—grandaunts, granduncles—kindly, tottering, near-death types who pass out and away now and then, leaving large sums of money to relations. None of my friends in New York had even one relative who died and left them money, and they thought I came from a fabulous family.

I was in with Tracy McVane's mother. If I could have lugged this swimming pool, this landscaping, and this house to school with me, who knows how many friends I could have picked up the first day? I think I was a little jealous of my mother and her ability to acquire friends. This house was far from the greatest in town—I knew that already—and it probably had nothing to do with my mother's popularity. *I* was the one who was making a case out of it.

"How was school? Nice teachers?" Mom asked. She didn't ask if I had made any friends. She wouldn't in front of these two women.

I shrugged. "Hard to tell the first day. Teachers are always making a presentation of themselves when school's new, under the guise of presenting the classwork. When the newness erodes, the real stuff emerges. Anyway, I think I can handle the work. And I met a few kids."

"In class?" Mom seemed uneasy about whether she should pursue this in front of her friends. She liked what I had said about the teachers. She had a wise daughter who knew the score.

I answered her question. "I met them in the cafeteria. A girl came up, introduced herself, and sat down. Then I met a couple of other kids through her."

"What's her name?" Epsy Tass asked.

"Elissa Hanes."

"A very smart girl. Brilliant, I hear."

Joanna McVane said, "Oh, yes, I know who she is. Very bright *but* . . ."

Mom looked perturbed. I had met a "but" girl the first day. "But what?" Mom was encouraging Joanna McVane.

"Nothing, really. Some of the high school girls say she's marginally flaky. Nothing serious."

"Marginally flaky. How so?" Mom asked.

How so from Mom meant drugs, sex, alcohol, orgies, stuff like that.

"She just talks kind of . . . kind of . . ."

"Only talk? That's it?" Mom didn't want to

hear anything else. Elissa had passed the Mom test. Flakiness, even if a communicable trait, would not get me pregnant, drunk, or spaced out.

I excused myself and went inside. I had homework to do. I wanted to start the year right scholastically. Socially, I wished I were back in New York. I wasn't the social star of my high school there, but I was comfortable with whatever I was. But that was all behind me and here I was in my new bedroom, at my new desk facing the mountains.

I concentrated on my homework. I liked my new room. I liked being alone. It made me feel honest. I knew that, along with the teachers, I had been trying to make a presentation of myself that first day. Not that I had said much. Elissa didn't give me a chance.

The telephone rang. It startled me. My telephone seemed to be more of a decoration than a functioning object. Nobody had telephoned me yet, except Mom and Dad when they were out and had something to tell me.

"Hello."

"Hi, Kim. This is Brett Fox. Remember me?"

"Of course not."

He was kidding, so I should kid back. That's normal. What wasn't normal was this phone call. He was calling me! He was shocking the socks off me.

"Can I refresh your memory by seeing you this Saturday night?"

"It might work."

"Pick you up at eight?"

"Fine. Do you know where I live? How did you get my telephone number? We're not in the book yet."

"Motivated people can get anything they want."

"That answer sounds like it has at least a dozen meanings. Does it?"

"Go out with me Saturday night and find out."

"Is this a challenge?"

What kind of guy was he anyway? Maybe I wouldn't like him when I went out with him. He seemed fine in the cafeteria, but maybe Brett Fox's ultimate shining moment had occurred over steakettes and string beans. Maybe he was the kind of guy who peaked in a crowded cafeteria, but get him alone and watch out. It bothered me that he had even marred his cafeteria image by describing Crystal Jameson as pretty. A guy sizing up a girl in front of other girls.

So what, *I* was the one he called for a date.

Unless he had called Crystal first.

There is a guard dog in my mind, digging

up trouble, creating pain, standing with teeth
bared between me and total euphoria. Out of
my way, dog. I've got a date with Brett Fox.
And I have a friend, Elissa Hanes. I'm doing
very well, possibly even knocking 'em dead,
as Dad had instructed.

Kim Adler, new girl in town, rejoice.

4

"So?"

This one word was my father's conversation opener at supper. He was better than my mother at asking questions. His one word conveyed everything. He was looking at me.

"Kim had lunch with a marginally flaky girl," my mother said as she passed the salad around.

"Good, good," Dad said. "Anything else?"

"I met a couple of guys," I said.

I figured that my parents would know about Brett sooner or later. After all, he was coming to the house Saturday night.

"Flaky too?"

"No. And Elissa's not flaky. Not exactly."

"I'm not sure I know what flaky means," Mom said.

"You're not supposed to know, dear," Dad said. He turned to me. "So?"

"One of the guys asked me out for Saturday night. Brett Fox, that's his name."

Dad whistled. "Not bad for your first day. What are you going to do for an encore?"

"Oh, Harris." Mom put her hand on my father's arm. But she looked pleased. "You feel as if you already belong, don't you Kim?" she asked.

"No."

"No?"

Mom was down to one-word questions.

"Mom, if you're a girl, the only way you really belong, I mean *really,* is if you're a member of this sorority they have. It's called Chi Kappa. Not that I want to be a member. I don't need that kind of belonging. It's not an official school club, anyway."

"Chi Kappa Sorority?" Dad was making cracking sounds as he ate a carrot. "What's that exactly?"

"Exactly it's a very exclusive group. They have only ten members at a time."

Dad stopped munching his carrot. "I don't believe in groups," he said. "I believe in one person, alone, a rugged individualist. Get two people together and it becomes conspiratorial. Three, and they have delusions of power. Four, and you've got the nucleus for taking over the world. Now *ten,* that's mind-boggling. They could destroy the universe."

My mother made a face. "Harris, don't joke. A sorority can be very important. Treat it with respect."

"Respect? That's a hallowed word. Don't throw it around. I love my work in advertising, but I don't respect it. I don't respect detergents, toothpaste, dandruff remover, dog food, and insect repellents, to name a few. You're talking to the man who dreamed up Pest-Off, something not quite worthy of reverence."

I laughed, almost choking on my salad. My father is an outspoken, irreverent man who creates hokum during his working hours and knocks it in his spare time. In New York he had a job dreaming up advertising campaigns for products. His biggest success was Pest-Off, an insect repellent. His new job in Palm Canyon was with a small advertising agency. He would probably never have a national hit like Pest-Off again, but he didn't care.

He turned to my mother. "Well, Claudine, how were things on the golf course? Any sororities forming there?"

I ate and listened while my parents talked. Someday what happens on the sixteenth or seventeenth fairway might grab me, but not right now. My head was already into the next day and what might happen at school.

The next day I got warm walking to school. I already knew that some of the kids in my area drove to school. They passed me by. I felt just as out of place as I had the day before. Here I was again, sallying forth into the land of strangers. I almost felt like a coward. Back in New York my friends and I pooled our cowardice when we were afraid of something, and we put up a brave collective front. But here I was alone. Or almost alone. I thought about Elissa and Brett and I felt better.

I had different classes today than I had yesterday. My day started a little later too. I had to get used to this system. I had missed Orientation Day, which would have clued me in to everything. And I might have met some strangers like myself. Still, I was able to find my classrooms without difficulty. After living in New York, you can find anything.

My clever analysis of teachers making presentations of themselves vanished when I met "Mrs. not Ms." Fontana, my English teacher. Her hair looked uncombed and she had a frantic way about her, as if she had rushed from home and forgotten to turn something off. Like the stove.

She tried to make the class feel comfortable by immediately launching into a discussion of Thoreau and his comment about hearing a different drummer. She wanted us to feel like individuals who were entitled to our idiosyncrasies and visions. The only problem with this approach was that I had heard it before. Also it doesn't necessarily make friends for you in the cafeteria, or anywhere else in school. I raised my hand, which seemed almost as bold an act as Elissa's arm waving the day before. Mrs. Fontana nodded for me to speak.

"Thoreau made another comment," I volunteered. "He said to beware of all enterprises that require new clothes. When you think about it, that's pretty solid advice. New clothes usually mean a new situation that you shouldn't go into blindly, without thought."

I sat there in the classroom and I knew what I was doing. *I* was making a presentation of myself. I was showing off, slightly. Some of the kids were giggling, but that didn't throw me off. I knew they would. But I wanted to be part of something, not an outsider. Now I was the most *in* student in the English class. I was the only one who had said anything so far. Maybe I was the only one wearing new clothes. I was being stared at. Some of the brighter kids might have guessed that my clothes were new, and might have wondered where I was coming from, psychologically and geographically.

"I'm going to like this class," Mrs. Fontana said.

It was a smart way of saying something nice about me without being too obvious. For someone whose house might be in flames now because of her haste, Mrs. Fontana still had her head on.

I got a few smiles from my classmates. I existed.

At lunch Elissa found me just as I was starting to eat. Once again she had doubles. Today's spread was a chili dog, pinto beans, coleslaw, and pineapple chunks. From the bite or two I had already taken, I thought the lunch was delicious. But it's not considered good form to say that school cafeteria lunches look good or taste good, so I kept quiet. Also, I didn't want to encourage Elissa in case she was tempted to take thirds.

"How's lunch?" she asked as she sat down.

"Could be worse," I said.

"What d'ya mean? This is the best food in town."

"You're not supposed to say that. What about home cooking? Don't you like what you get at home?"

"My mom doesn't cook," Elissa said. She was stirring her coleslaw as if it were soup. "My father doesn't cook, either, but that doesn't matter because he doesn't live with us. He's remarried. Mom and I live alone. I've got a little brother, but he lives with my father. The divorce judge believed in breaking up families, I guess."

"He did?"

"She. The judge was a lady. Maybe she sized up Mom as the nondomestic type.

Maybe the judge went home at the end of a long day of sitting on that bench and opened cans and TV dinners, and when she saw Mom she recognized a kindred nondomestic spirit. Little boys, still growing up, are entitled to more than cans and TV dinners. We had a cook when Mom and Dad were married. She left when they split."

"She had split loyalties?" I hadn't meant to make a pun.

"I wouldn't call it that. She left to marry my father. Anyway, you're not interested in my family's business. You're wondering if Brett is going to come along, aren't you?"

"Well . . ."

"He might have brought his lunch and be eating it outside with some of the guys. Lots of kids eat outside. Also, this school has shifts, and he could be on a different lunch shift today. You'll see him again, I guarantee it."

"I know I'll see him again. He asked me out for this Saturday night. He phoned me yesterday right after I got home."

Elissa's coleslaw survived its stirring. She was eating it. "That's *terrific*, Kim," she said. "I love to see new alliances formed."

"New alliances?"

"Sure. He's new in school and you're new in school, and new kids deserve some of the power. Stick together and maybe you'll get it."

"But we're just a girl and a guy going out on a date. We don't have any power."

Elissa's chili dog was gone before she answered. "Brett's very tall and very good-looking, and I predict that pretty soon he'll be a big shot in the school. You're extremely interesting-looking—thin body, thick, incredible hair. Maybe you and Brett will become the killer couple."

If I turned and looked at Elissa, I was sure I'd see her future face again. Elissa was a strategist. She seemed to do things spontaneously, but there were blueprints in her mind. Epsy Tass had said she was brilliant. Joanna McVane had said she was marginally flaky. Now I preferred to believe flaky. Flaky I could deal with, but blueprint brilliance was something else.

"Don't look up," Elissa said suddenly, causing me to look up. My eyes swept over the room. I saw Buckingham Palace, where Rona Dunne and Tracy McVane were sitting with two girls who looked identical. I also recognized Eric Day, who was sitting at a distant table. For Elissa's sake I wished he would come over today. Then I saw Brett, standing with Crystal Jameson. She was looking up at him, which is the only way most girls could look at his face. He must be six four, six five, six six?

They were holding trays and talking. I guess I caught Brett's eye because he walked toward my table. Crystal kept up with him. He arrived. Crystal arrived. "Hi, Kim, hi, Elissa," he said. Crystal stood beside him. Now that she was up close I could see what she really looked like. She had soft, pink skin like a baby's, an upward tilting optimistic nose, a matching turned-up optimistic mouth, and the meanest eyes I had ever seen. You could pick and choose from her features and expressions and believe what you wanted about her.

Brett introduced Crystal to me, while Crystal gazed at him worshipfully. When had he met her, I wondered. Just now? Yesterday? Or in some sort of prenatal match made in heaven?

"Get acquainted, girls," Brett said. "I'm eating with the guys today. Have fun."

He walked off, eluding Crystal, but eluding me too. He had treated me like one of the girls, not someone he had asked for a date. But really, what was there to say in front of Crystal and Elissa?

Crystal sat down opposite us. She was wearing a tan dress tied around the middle with a tan rope.

"Your chili dog and pinto beans must be cold by now, Crystal," Elissa remarked. It was a tricky comment. It was like saying that Crystal and Brett must have been standing and talking together for some time over an increasingly cool lunch. Was Elissa hoping for more information?

Crystal tried a couple of beans. "Warm enough," she said casually.

"How long have you known Brett?" Elissa asked.

"Not long. But we have something in common."

Did Crystal come from New York too? I didn't want her to come from New York. It was dumb to not want that, but that's the way it was. I hoped she was one of the Minnesota people Elissa had mentioned the day before. Come from Minnesota, Crystal.

It didn't matter where she came from. She wasn't talking geography. She was talking height. She said, "Brett is six feet four and so is my dad."

"Fantastic," Elissa said. "Just fantastic."

Elissa didn't mean fantastic. She meant stupid. It was there in her voice. But Crystal ignored the scorn. "If you had a father six feet four, you'd know what I mean," she said.

"My father *is* six feet four," Elissa said airily.

I didn't believe her. Anyway, her father

wasn't around for anyone to check it out. Elissa was baiting Crystal. But Crystal didn't care. She wanted us to know something. She was leading up to it.

"You know," she said, looking straight at me, "it's hard to find presents for somebody that big. I mean, you buy something and then it doesn't fit so you have to take it back."

"I know," Elissa said, with sympathy in her voice. "Shaving lotion, stereo tapes, a book, a briefcase, they never seem to fit. Awful problem."

Crystal went sailing on. "Dad's birthday is next week and I want to get him one of those western shirts I see around town. Brett offered to help me, like trying on the shirts in the store to see if they'd fit such a big frame."

"He *offered?*" Elissa lost her cool. "Guys don't like to go shopping. They hate it."

"I *know,*" Crystal said, as she dug into her food. She had an appetite. She had just won the conversation.

Elissa hadn't conceded. "Tell me," she said. "What happens if Brett has one muscle—or sinew or bone or blood vessel or whatever—different from your father's?"

"He doesn't. Brett and my father are identical. Giants!"

I had never seen Crystal's father. But suddenly I had a clear vision of him. He was four

feet ten and weighed fifty-seven pounds. A
tight, scrawny little man, with shoulders nar-
row and stooped, causing him to look like he
had spent his life bent over a desk adding up
and scratching out figures for a living. He
could alternately be described as frail, petite,
wizened, shriveled, and at death's door.

Elissa chewed her pineapple chunks. "Why
are you telling us all of this, Crystal?"

"You asked about Brett, remember?"

That wasn't the reason. That was the excuse. Crystal's Information Booth had opened
for my benefit. She was telling *me* about
Brett.

"Lots of luck on your shopping expedition,"
Elissa said. She wanted to close the subject.

Crystal wasn't ready to shut down. She said,
"Thanks. It should be a fun afternoon this Saturday."

This Saturday? Brett was taking me out Saturday night. Now Saturday night was tainted.
Brett would go from Crystal to me. A split
Saturday. Had he really offered to go shopping with Crystal or had she asked him?

Crystal was smiling sweetly across the table
at me. Read Crystal's lips: innocence. Read
Crystal's eyes: a dark plan unfolding. She finished her meal silently, stood up, said "See
you guys," took her tray, and walked out of
sight.

"Whew!" I said. "You two are crazy about each other. Stop me if I'm wrong."

"Keep going," Elissa said. "She's from somewhere in Florida. I met her last winter, the first day she came to school. From the beginning she was sweetly hostile, and that's the worst kind of hostility."

The first day she came to school. Had Elissa gone up to Crystal? Was this a pattern? Crystal must have rejected Elissa. Otherwise, why the hostility now from Elissa?

"Let's just eat," I said. "That's what the cafeteria is for, isn't it?"

It wasn't. Halfway through my pineapple chunks, Tracy McVane left Buckingham Palace and walked across the cafeteria to my table. She bent down and tapped me lightly on the shoulder. "Kim Adler?" she said. "I'm Tracy McVane. Care to join my friends and me at our table?"

5

Did the invitation include Elissa?

It had *better* include Elissa. I didn't need any more hostility.

I was still angry about Crystal and Brett. But there wasn't anything I could do about them, was there? I gave Tracy a look that was inspired by what had just happened.

Tracy looked puzzled. "Kim, my mother met your mother, and Mom suggested that I introduce you around." Tracy hesitated. "I guess you already know everybody, Elissa."

"All too well," Elissa murmured.

"Elissa and I would love to join you," I said. I stood up and accidentally bumped into Tracy. "Sorry," I said. I grabbed Elissa's tray and started to carry it toward Buckingham Palace. Elissa shrugged, took my tray, and followed me. Tracy followed Elissa.

There were three girls at the sorority table. Tracy introduced me to Rona Dunne and the Baron twins, Daisy and Tulip. Somebody must have liked flowers in the Baron family. The twins' faces looked almost identical except that Daisy wore glasses and Tulip didn't. Tulip probably wore contacts. If you stared at the twins, which I did, you'd notice that Tulip tried a little harder than her twin. Tulip's hair and makeup were more carefully done. Rona Dunne was blond-perfect, and that about took care of that. No qualifiers. Tracy McVane surprisingly looked the flashiest of the four. Being the editor of the school newspaper carries with it a promise of seriousness and good taste. Sometimes it's only a promise. Yesterday wasn't her hair sort of brown? Today Tracy was wearing garish orange lipstick, and her hair was colored to match in a pink-orange sort of way. I bet she and her mother fought over that. Joanna McVane was tasteful.

I turned to see if I could catch an expression on Elissa's face. But there was nothing revealing. Elissa at Buckingham Palace. It had happened. I wondered if all eyes were on us in the cafeteria. Crystal Jameson had left. Too bad.

Elissa, Tracy, and I sat down. I was glad that Elissa had finished one of her meals. Two meals at a time wouldn't have gone over well with the members of Chi Kappa. Not that Elissa or I cared. Or maybe I did because I wouldn't have thought of that if I didn't. Elissa must have thought of it, too, because she had managed to dump the plastic container that her first meal had come in.

I didn't have anything much to eat, actually. My pineapple chunks were down to two.

But Tracy McVane kept me busy. She served me up to the other girls, you might say. "Kim moved here from New York, New York," Tracy began.

Tulip Baron picked it up from there. "Why did you move here when all the action is back east?"

"Too much action, I guess. I mean, for my folks. Too much weather . . . cold weather. And New York is a very fast-paced city."

"You didn't like it?" Daisy picked up from her sister. Why did I have the feeling that this was like a quiz where there is actually a wrong answer and a right answer?

Rona didn't give me a chance to answer that one. She asked, "What do you think of Palm Canyon?"

"Well, aside from occasional snakes, relentlessly hot weather, the world's largest supply of continuously barking dogs, barren landscapes that don't look good barren and don't look good when the hotshot developers build on them either, it's fine. On the plus side I think winter is going to be very pleasant here, and I can live out my entire life in nice, airy, comfortable sandals, and not worry about being asked to shovel snow. So there are pluses and minuses."

I was going on and on and on. Why? Was I showing off for these girls? Was I auditioning for them? Maybe I wanted something that I didn't want to want. Or maybe I was just nervous.

Elissa was eating fiendishly. She and her food were as one. For the moment. She finished her lunch, looked up at Tracy McVane, and said, "Nice dye job."

This was it. The end. Elissa had a big mouth. I had liked it when it worked in my favor but now it was getting destructive.

But Tracy McVane was grinning. "You really like it? Mom detests it but she says it's an improvement over last week's purple."

Tracy was proud of her horrible hair, and I guess Elissa knew it. Elissa said, "The green last month was really you. It takes guts to go green."

Elissa was playing up to Tracy. Did Elissa want something she didn't want to want?

Rona was looking me over. "I understand that your father was a top copywriter for a top advertising agency in New York. He . . ."

Tracy broke in. "I told Rona. Your Mom told my Mom. He did Pest-Off, Rona. I forgot to tell you that."

"Pest-Off? That's famous," Rona said. "We actually bought some on the basis of seeing those commercials. We really need that stuff out here. We seem to have everything that crawls."

Elissa was about to comment on that, but thought better of it. She was on her best behavior, and it somehow bothered me. She knew she was at this table only because I had included her. She was looking around the room from her new vantage point. She stopped, fixing her eyes on a table near us. Eric Day was sitting there, facing us. I understood. Elissa was temporarily enshrined among royalty and it couldn't hurt for Eric to know it. Eric noticed. He raised his arm and kind of saluted Elissa.

Elissa abruptly stood up. There was plenty of her old independence left. She was leaving the table voluntarily, on her own. "Gotta run. See you later, Kim," she said. She nodded to the other girls and left without taking her tray. I think it was on purpose. The sorority girls were left with Elissa's messy tray. They could endure it, or become her garbage crew by dumping her trash and depositing her tray.

I was on my own. "Do you have any favorite hobbies?" Rona asked.

What do you call a person who is quizzed for fifteen minutes straight? A quizee? An idiot for allowing it? As soon as Elissa left, the questions flew thick and fast at me. Rona, Tracy, and the flower twins wanted to know

everything. It felt like a high-powered inter-
view, the kind my father talks about.

What were the other sorority members
like? These girls were keeping me too busy to
ask. Rona was the president. She was cool, and
the elegant lady she would someday become
was already seeping through. She wasn't
stuck-up, but she seemed to put a little space
between herself and the other girls, including
me. She could afford the space because she
was so popular. Most of us don't have that
luxury. We have to be accessible. We have to
show that we're available for friendship,
dates, confidences, shared secrets, and anything else that makes us part of the scene.

I wondered if Brett was watching me at the
sorority table, and I hated myself for wondering. He had said he was going to sit with some
guys. I couldn't see him.

I was getting a new picture of myself. As
someone coveted, desirable. All the questions
from the girls that had annoyed me were settling into my head as something quite wonderful. They were so interested in me. Therefore, I must be interesting.

At last lunch was over, and we all got up to
leave. Rona said, "Come sit with us tomorrow
and meet some of the other girls, Kim."

My mind flashed ahead to the next day.
Elissa would look for me. Elissa would want to

sit with me. But if I sat with Elissa every day it would become an established routine or something, and I might cut myself off from meeting other kids. Unless Elissa went into her arm-waving maneuver, which could get sticky if repeated too much. Elissa had befriended me, but the sorority girls must like me too. They must see something in me to ask me to sit with them again. One solution was to avoid Elissa *and* the sorority girls by bringing my lunch the next day and eating it outside picnic fashion like a lot of kids do. How had I gotten into this? What did I owe Elissa?

I felt a combination of pain and confusion. I felt torn. But somehow I said "Great" to the sorority girls.

6

After lunch I decided that I didn't like my French teacher. If French class had been before lunch maybe I would have liked the teacher. That's the kind of mixed-up mood I was in. Sorry about that, Mr. Middle. Mr. Middle didn't seem like a good name for a French teacher. It didn't seem like a good name for a teacher period. It rhymed with things. Like riddle and fiddle and who knows what. I believe that no one with a rhyming name should go into teaching. It tempts kids. Mrs. Fontana rhymed with Montana. I started to think rhymes instead of French. Fox rhymes with pox, and I'll graduate from high school when I'm ninety if I don't stop this.

Elissa caught up with me on my way home from school. It was the first time I had ever really noticed her walk. Elissa moved like someone who had mistakenly enrolled in a ballet class and was futilely trying to master the steps. Maybe it had something to do with her weight and maybe it didn't. I wanted to help her with her walk. I wanted to help her with anything I could. I felt guilty about the sorority. In the instant that I saw her trying to catch up with me, I wondered if walking home from school with her every day might become a habit just like eating lunch together. I hadn't even walked home with her one time and yet I was thinking this. I felt rotten for worrying about it. I had wanted a friend desperately. I had one. And I knew I couldn't afford the luxury of distancing myself from anyone. I wasn't Rona Dunne.

"I live just a few blocks from you," Elissa said. "I told you that yesterday, didn't I?"

"No."

"Well, I do. I live where the acre lots stop and the condos begin. Mom and I have a condo. Come home with me and meet Mom."

Elissa was eager. She must be proud of her mother. I was a little curious. But I would be cementing the friendship. I had a right to go slowly.

"My mother will be looking for me," I said.

"Call her from my place," Elissa said. And that was that.

I didn't know what to expect. Mothers of girls come in several categories. My mother doesn't want me to associate with anyone who's hazardous to my health or morality. That's about it. But some mothers are very competitive. They want their daughters to associate with Popularity in case it rubs off or they want their daughters to associate with

Unpopularity so that their daughters, by comparison, might shine.

Elissa's mother didn't fall into any category that I could peg. When I met her I was too stunned to think about categories anyway. She was skinny. I mean skinny. Much thinner than me. She was dressed in a dazzling white suit. And the condo was smashing. The living room was all in peach and white: fluffy carpeting, sofa, chairs. There were touches of chrome, and gorgeous greenery. Elissa lived Hollywood-style. She gave me a tour. There were two all-in-white bedrooms, and a tiny kitchen done in peach and white. The small bathroom was also peach and white. The place wasn't nearly as big as it seemed. It wasn't big at all. It was clever.

Elissa's mother was watching a game show on TV when we walked in. Elissa introduced us briefly. She didn't want to disturb her mother. Her mother gave me a warm, slightly vacant smile and went back to the game show. Afterwards I realized I'd have to invent a mother category for her. Oblivious Mom.

After the tour Elissa took me to her bedroom. It had a bed, a glass-topped white desk, and a bookcase made of white cane and glass. The bookcase was full of books. The desk was dominated by a framed picture of a young boy. Most likely Elissa's brother. Paintings of

birds were on the walls. No posters. A room
without posters has no real personality. A few
obnoxious posters tell you that the room's occupant will follow the herd, will scream in
admiration at a no-talent jerk, and will be
begging for an advance on next month's al-
lowance to buy more trivia. Elissa did not
have normal teen walls. Her walls were into
middle age.

"Fabulous condo," I said.

"Yeah, isn't it," Elissa said. She pointed to a
white telephone on her desk. "It's all yours.
You wanted to let your mother know where
you are."

"Right."

I dialed my number. It was strange having
this new number as my home number. My
mother answered immediately. She was up-
set. The moment I said "Hi, Mom," she said,
"You were supposed to come straight home.
We both have an appointment with the dentist, remember? This is a fine way to start off a
relationship."

I never think of what I have with a dentist
as being a relationship. My dentist in New
York gave me the creeps. He had new equipment every time I went there, and I went
there every six months. No cavities. Just
cleaning and an examination and a look at
what was new in space-age dentistry. Not

only was he equipment-crazy, he sent engraved bills. I know because my mother loathes engraved bills. But she admires new equipment. She says it's a sign that a dentist is up on things. Now she was prepared for this new relationship with someone who had been recommended by a stranger on the golf course.

I told my mother I'd be right home. I hung up and said to Elissa, "I've got a dentist appointment. Forgot all about it."

"Go," she said. "Mustn't be late for all that excitement."

Elissa didn't seem disappointed to see me go. I had seen what she had wanted me to see. Her thin mother, her fluffy peach-and-white condo. I waved to her mother as I left, but her mother was watching a jumping, hand-clapping, shrieking contestant who had answered a question correctly and had obviously just won the world.

It was too hot to rush home but I rushed anyway. I went directly to the bathroom, where I brushed my teeth. Mom always insists that I clean my teeth before I go to the dentist to have them cleaned. I was sure she had already brushed hers. She was in the den putting on our telephone-answering machine, the last thing she does when we leave the house empty.

"Let's go," she said to me as I rinsed my toothbrush. "We'll just make it."

The telephone rang.

Mom opened the front door.

"Let's answer it," I said. Brett could be calling. I hoped not. Our date was set.

"No time," Mom said as Dad's recorded announcement started to play. Mom and I left the house to the sound of his voice: *This is the Adler family—Harris, Claudine, and Kim. We are unable to come to the telephone. At the sound of the beep, please leave a brief message. We will not return long-distance calls unless you are phoning from an Unidentified Flying Object or there's money in it for us.*

The dentist made us wait three quarters of an hour. My mother always forgave doctors who made her wait, and she was now extending the same courtesy to her new dentist. She was brought up to believe that The Dentist is "your good friend" along with The Doctor, The Policeman, The Teacher, and the President of the United States. All I could think of was getting back to the telephone-answering machine and finding out who called. Maybe I had a broken date.

The dentist didn't find any cavities in my mother or me and we were out of there pretty fast with our gleaming minty bright teeth. Mom stopped along the way home to pick up some groceries.

Finally I was reunited with the answering machine. There had been only one call. Mom was putting away the groceries, so she told me to let her know who it was. It was probably one of her new friends. I had overreacted to the call.

The voice of Sidney Megovitch erupted into the den. "Hi, Kim. Hi, Mrs. Adler. Hi, Mr. Adler. You're not home, Kim? How's the weather out there? I have to talk to you. Very imp—"

Message time was over. Poor Sidney. He didn't know how to be brief or concise. Now what? Should I call him back? I didn't want to encourage him, but I didn't want to be rude either. Actually I felt pretty good about his calling. None of my other friends from New York had phoned. They didn't come from families like Sidney's, though. His parents could afford anything and everything. I decided that they could spring for another long-distance phone call. I'd just wait for Sidney to call me back. One problem solved.

I ran my tongue over my teeth. They felt smooth and clean. No cavities once again. Then I thought, if the dentist was really a good friend, as in my mother's childhood indoctrination, he would have found a bunch of cavities in my mouth and ordered me to abstain from eating for a week.

That way I wouldn't have to show up for lunch at school tomorrow and make a decision I didn't want to make.

7

The sorority table was empty when I got to the cafeteria the next day. I had brought my lunch in a small bag from home. I didn't have to carry a tray around. This gave me an odd feeling of mobility, of mastery over my fate. In my mind I had already mastered my fate. Finally I had everything figured out. I would sit with the sorority girls and when Elissa came into the cafeteria and looked around for me I would beckon her to the sorority table. If the sorority girls didn't like it, tough luck.

I practically ran from my last class to the cafeteria. I wanted to beat Elissa there. Usually I showed up before she did, but I had to make sure. I seemed to have beat the sorority girls too. I sat down at their empty table, my unopened lunch bag in front of me. I kept looking at the entrance to the cafeteria. I wished my plan had happened already.

I saw Brett come into the cafeteria. Maybe I could wave him over. A guy at the sorority table. Why not? I felt like making waves. For the moment the sorority table was mine, all mine. Then I saw Crystal Jameson. She was behind Brett. She was beside Brett. She was with Brett. At a distance I didn't know what was going on, but then I saw them walk to a table and sit down together. I don't think Brett saw me. Brett was more important to me than the sorority. So why was I sitting here instead of with him? Crystal knew how to grab him before he sat down. Maybe it was as simple as that. Maybe it wasn't. Tomorrow night was my date with him. Tomorrow afternoon was hers.

Brett was facing me. He saw me. I felt important. I felt stupid. What if he thought I wasn't *asked* to sit at this table? What if he thought I was throwing myself at the sorority girls? He smiled at me and I smiled back.

I almost forgot about Elissa. Then I saw her. She already had her tray. I waved to her. I beckoned to her. I must have looked like a drowning person. Frantic. I was sending out two messages: I'm at the sorority table, I want you to join me. She waved back as best she could while holding her full tray. Then she walked over to a table where two other girls were sitting and she sat down and joined them.

I couldn't believe it! She turned down a chance to eat at the sorority table. She also turned down a chance to have lunch with me. She hadn't hesitated. And here I was worrying about offending *her*.

I opened my lunch bag. It looked sort of

tiny and pitiful. Maybe *I* did. I couldn't just sit
and watch for the sorority girls. I had to do
something. Eating seemed logical. I took a
bite out of my cheese sandwich. I shouldn't
have brought cheese, the hot weather and all.
It wasn't spoiled but it wasn't in top shape
either. I thought about different kinds of
cheeses because I didn't want to think about
my situation. I was ten or fifteen minutes into
thinking about cheeses when I realized that I
had eaten my sandwich, eaten my figs, eaten
my cookies, and nobody had showed up at the
table. I must have been the star attraction in
the cafeteria, the lone occupant at a table that
sits at least a dozen. I was either the star jerk
or the star star. I mean I had Buckingham
Palace all to myself. I was the queen, you
might say. But I must have looked like a con-
taminated queen, with nobody, absolutely nobody, sitting with me. Where were the sorority girls? I didn't see Tracy or Rona or Carrie
Reis or the flower twins anywhere in the cafeteria, and I didn't know the other members
by sight. Was this situation inflicted on me or
did I inflict it on myself?

I brushed my crumbs into my lunch bag. I
crumpled my wax paper and put it in the bag.
I crumpled the bag and took it to the trash
bin.

I left the cafeteria.

8

Tulip Baron, the twin who tried harder, was waiting for me outside the classroom after my last period of the day.

"Were we supposed to meet you at lunch?" she asked.

Didn't she *know?*

"Yeah," I said casually.

"That's what I thought. That's what we all thought. That is, Rona, Tracy, and my sister and I. We were outside at lunch. An emergency came up, a sorority thing we had to discuss. We finally got to the cafeteria, but late. And we're very sorry. Did you eat?"

"Yes."

"I hope you had company."

"At the sorority table? How could I?"

"The sorority doesn't own the table. The cafeteria gets crowded and sometimes we do get outsiders. That is, non-sorority members sitting there. Anyway, we're really sorry and we hope you'll eat with us some other time."

"Well, okay."

What else could I say? The apology sounded sincere. It was full of holes, of course. Why couldn't one of the members have come and told me they'd be late? Also it seemed to me that the reason they had to meet outside to discuss "a sorority thing" was because they remembered they had invited a non-sorority member to join them at their table. An apology with holes in it was probably worse than no apology at all, but Tulip's stab at being thoughtful and polite worked. It worked against logic.

Tulip dashed off, mission accomplished.

I walked home by myself. A girl from my English class passed me by and said hi. I said hi back and that was it. I was glad to be leaving school for the weekend. I was looking forward to Saturday night.

I picked out old clothes to wear on my date. Mr. Thoreau would have approved. Or would he? I was missing the point of what he had said. This enterprise probably did require new clothes. I just wasn't wearing them. I picked a green dress with a matching jacket that my father had bought for me a year ago. My father buys my clothes sometimes. He has more flair and imagination than my mother. We all know that.

The next day I allowed myself a few hours to get ready, including a leisurely soak in our big Roman tub. Enclosed in its wonderful sunken splendor, I stretched out and felt guilty. I thought about my granduncle Fraser Adler, also stretched out, in a manner of speaking, who had passed away and left us enough money for items like this fabulous tub. We should put a dignified little plaque with his name on it over the tub and other various luxurious items in our house that Uncle Fraser had paid for post-mortem. My father's good job in New York afforded us a lot of nice things, but we have more nice things than his job afforded us. And now his salary is so-so.

While I soaked I wondered if Brett was finished being a model for Crystal. They could still be together united in a quest for a western shirt for Crystal's midget father. Brett might show up late for our date. I didn't feel an urgency about getting dressed. I would be ready on time at eight, and not before.

The green dress looked better than ever. Old clothes reach a point where one day they're fine and the next day they're history, but this green number went on and on. I don't wear much makeup and my hair takes care of itself. It looks great without even combing it or brushing it. I was almost ready for Brett. Impulsively I put on something new. Green sandals. Dad had insisted that they went perfectly with the dress. We had been shopping in a mall, and he saw them in a window. He said they were the same green as my dress. I have no memory for matching colors in my head but he does. We took the shoes home and held them up to the dress, and they looked like they were from the same dye lot. By eight o'clock, between my dress, my shoes, and my hair I was a golden and green person, ready to meet the world, namely Brett. I expected him to be late, which seemed more sensible than expecting him to be on time and then getting disappointed.

At eight o'clock sharp a bell rang. But it didn't belong to the front door. It belonged to the telephone. "I'll get it!" I called. Brett was probably calling to say he'd be late. I was nicely prepared. I was one girl who wasn't going to be disappointed.

I picked up the receiver. "Hello."

"Kim?"

"Yes."

He sounded young and eager over the phone. He hadn't sounded so young that first time on the phone, when he called to ask for this date.

"I see you know who this is," he went on.

All at once I didn't know who it was.

"This is Sidney," the voice said as the front doorbell rang.

"Sidney. Oh, Sidney. Hi. Uh, someone's at my front door."

My father called to me. "I'll get it, Kim."

It must be Brett! Exactly on time! I was torn

two ways. Sidney was calling again long-distance. But my date was at the door.

"Sidney," I said. "It's just great hearing from you. Sorry I wasn't home when you called. Everything's fine here. I guess you were just checking in across the miles to say hi. Well hi there. Tell you what. Next time I'll phone you, okay? And look, give my best to your parents and Shannon and all the gang. I really appreciate the call, Sidney."

"Appreciate it longer. Keep talking."

"But this call must be costing a fortune. New York to Arizona."

"A fortune? This is the weekend. Cheapie time rates. Anyway, what do my folks care."

I heard my front door open and close and my father saying "You must be Brett."

If my father was feeling creative, playful, there was no telling what he would say to Brett. Sometimes Dad embarrassed Mom and me. Like that telephone machine message. When Mom got a chance to record, she was all business. She asked the caller to please leave a name and number and that was it. Dad was usually content to ask my dates traditional questions that he already knew the answers to. Like what year are you in at school, what's your favorite subject, how do you think the team—whatever the team was—is doing this year? But at other times Dad was not above saying "I hope you're not fast, young man. Just remember . . . your date has a father."

Brett and Dad must have gone into the living room. I couldn't hear their conversation. I hoped Mom wouldn't join them. Two parents —practically a committee—sizing up Brett.

"You there, Kim?"

Sidney was waiting.

"I'm here. It's just that I . . . well, I have a date tonight and he just showed up. It's eight o'clock in Palm Canyon, on a Saturday night. What time is it where you are?"

"You've got a date so soon?"

I didn't mean to hurt Sidney. But I had a right to go out.

"He's somebody from school. I don't know where we're going, but he could have tickets for something and if I stay on the phone we'll be late. How about my calling you back tomorrow?"

"Good. Maybe you'll have an answer to my question. The one I haven't asked yet. See, my folks are going to Palm Springs, California, for Thanksgiving and they thought they'd drop me off along the way to spend a couple of days in Palm Canyon. Two Palms, Canyon and Springs. Isn't it a coincidence?"

"Are they driving? I don't think Palm Canyon is on the way to Palm Springs."

"We're flying. They're dropping me off in

Chicago. That is, I'll switch to another flight and my folks will go on to Palm Springs. So would you like a guest for Thanksgiving?"

Sidney's parents unload Sidney and his sister whenever possible. They love their kids and they're loved back, and it's all incredible because a dumped kid is usually an unloved or nuisance kid. Not so in the Megovitch family.

"What about your sister? What's she going to do?" I asked, evading the question of Sidney's visit.

"We have a cousin in Chicago whom Shannon hasn't seen for three or four weeks, so Shannon's spending Thanksgiving there. My folks are dropping her off, too, on their way to Palm Springs."

What was going on in my living room? Our house is all on one level, except for the guest quarters in the basement, but still I couldn't hear the living room conversation. *The guest quarters!* We had room for Sidney. I couldn't say that we didn't. I just couldn't pull something like that on Sidney.

"I'll have to check this out with my parents," I said finally. This would give me time to think. Sidney in Palm Canyon. A whole Thanksgiving of being worshiped. But by Thanksgiving I might be able to get my worshiping from another, older, more exciting source.

"Sure," Sidney said. "Check it out. Can I call you back in a few days? I don't want you to pay for calls because you're doing me the favor by having me as your Thanksgiving guest."

It sounded settled. Sidney wasn't a con artist, trying to slickslide a possibility into a fact. This was just the way his mind worked. If an idea struck him as being okay, well that made it okay. It would happen because it was a Megovitch-approved idea.

"Fine, call me next week," I said. Did I mean fine that he was coming for Thanksgiving or fine that he should call me next week? Who knows anymore. I just had to get off th phone. What was Brett thinking in the living room? Was he squirming?

"When next week? What day? What time your time?"

"Uh, early evening. Um, say Wednesday. All right?"

"Super. I'm sure glad I caught you tonight. Think about me when you're out on your date."

"I'm thinking of you and I'm not out on it yet. I'll speak to you Wednesday, Sidney. Okay? We're all set on that?"

Oh, let this conversation be *over*. I can't wound Sidney, but enough is enough.

"Until Wednesday, Kim," he said softly.

"Until Wednesday," I said.

I hung up and looked in the mirror. I was sure the conversation had changed my appearance. My soak in the tub had been canceled out and I felt hot and sweaty. But I looked the same. I grabbed my purse and walked quickly into the living room.

Brett and my father were sitting and laughing. At least it wasn't one of those "Yes, sir, my intentions toward your daughter are strictly honorable" kind of atmospheres, where the guy is proper and stiff and phony.

Brett stood up when he saw me. He took in my golden-green look and appeared to like it. I said, "I'm awfully sorry I'm late. I got a long-distance phone call just as you rang our bell. The same person phoned me before and missed me and, well, it's hard to ask a person to call a third time."

"I know," Brett said. "I get calls from New York and I hate to miss them. Part of my life is still there. You feel the same way?"

The only feeling I had right now was toward Brett. He was understanding, he was tall, he was wearing a blue shirt that brought out the brown in his eyes. How could that be?

"Hey, kids," my father said. "You're going to be late for wherever you're going. Come on, get out of here."

"Yes, sir, Dad," I said. "See you later."

"Nice meeting you, Mr. Adler. Hope to see you again."

"You will," Dad answered.

They shook hands.

Dad's and Brett's first date was a resounding success. Now it was my turn.

9

We walked to Brett's car. That's when I realized he had one. That's when I realized he must be at least sixteen or he couldn't have a driver's license. That's when I realized that I didn't know if he was a junior or a senior or what. He loomed up in the darkness beside me, almost bigger than life. In the dark his size made him look like a formidable aggressor or a formidable protector.

He opened the car door for me. It looked like an expensive car. If it belonged to Brett's parents they must be fairly well off, but if it belonged to Brett alone his parents must be very well off to buy it for him. Unless they went into hock like most of America. I usually don't think about things like this, but everything about Brett interested me. As I eased into the front seat I saw that it was kind of plush. A nice place to sit and get kissed. I usually don't think about things like *this* at the beginning of a first date either.

"Your father's quite a guy," he said as we drove off.

"Isn't he. I hope you didn't mind his keeping you company while I was on the phone."

"Not at all. I'm sorry I didn't get to meet your mother too."

He wanted to meet my family! Could he mean it? It was kind of old-fashioned, square, and romantic.

"Next time," I said boldly.

"Do you have any brothers or sisters?" he asked.

"No. Do you?"

"A sister. She's a freshman. She's in luck, I guess. She didn't have to switch high schools in midstream. She can go to Palm Canyon High for all four years."

"What year are you in, Brett?"

"I'm a senior. And you're a junior?"

"How did you know?" I hoped he did plenty of checking up on me. I hoped he wanted to know every last little thing there was to know about me. I hoped he didn't find out everything. The looking was what counted.

He answered my question. "You must have mentioned it," he said. "Or maybe it was Elissa Hanes or Crystal Jameson. Somebody."

"Crystal Jameson? She told you about me?"

"Yeah, she told me some things. She's a real fan of yours. I'd be flattered if I were you."

I wasn't flattered.

"You and she went shopping for a shirt for her father?"

"For about four hours. Crystal couldn't make up her mind. She had me trying on one shirt after another. I'll never do that again, and I don't know why I did it this time, but she is just the sweetest. It's hard to turn down someone like her. A person you'd practically roll over and die for. What more can I say?"

Say no more, I thought. Crystal had made a friend of Brett. Not a boyfriend, it seemed. Not at this stage. She knew what she was doing. *First* a friend, *then* a boyfriend. A natural evolution if done properly.

We stopped talking for a while as we drove along. This was my first date in the Southwest, my first date among the palm trees and the saguaro cactus and the desert brush. But as we went nearer to the heart of town we entered some bad neighborhoods. Or perhaps they were just sad neighborhoods. Some of them might be called traditional neighborhoods because the houses have been around so long, but I felt that the people were living there not because of a love of tradition but because of a lack of money. The residents don't truly *live* there, they are left behind there. Mom says that when I get married she wants me to live in a house that's my choice and not my fate. Every time we went through a poor neighborhood in New York I knew what she was talking about. I had never seen this poor side of Palm Canyon. It was basically a well-heeled community. Suddenly I wondered if Brett lived here and was taking me home to meet his family. He seemed like a family meeter. Maybe this car was the only expensive item in his family. Then I remembered that he had said his mother had a good job.

"Where are we going?" I asked.

"Oh, I didn't tell you? I mean, ask you? I meant to. I thought we'd take in a play downtown. Do you like the theater?"

"Yes," I said. I do, but I would have said yes anyway.

"This is a production by a local theatrical group and they're not bad. It's not New York, understand, but what is? This theater is located on Palm Canyon's off Broadway, you might say. Just south of downtown. The neighborhood's not the best, but the theater's quite nice inside. Renovated."

The neighborhood was getting more commercial. It wasn't any better than the residential section we had just left, but it was trying harder. Small shops, more lights, more people. One of those tacky-trying-to-get-artsy areas that would probably become a tourist mecca by next year.

Brett found a parking place on a side street. We got out of the car. I wasn't afraid of the neighborhood with his six-four height towering beside me.

The first act was well under way when we were ushered to our seats. It was my fault that we were late, but Brett didn't say a word about it. The play was a production of something I had seen on Broadway a couple of years ago. This local company was quite solid, and the inside of the theater was attractive. It was the jewel of the neighborhood, one of those surprises you get when you find that the inside of a building is totally at odds with the outside. I felt sorry for the lady sitting behind Brett. I'd hate to sit behind anyone that tall in a theater. You can ask a person to remove a hat but not a head.

There was a love scene in the play. Brett just stared straight ahead and watched it. I put myself in the scene with Brett. I kept thinking about the front seat of his car. I didn't want to participate in a sizzling love scene there, but I wondered if he was going to kiss me in his car. Would I let him? Of course I would. But I couldn't be too anxious. He might get the wrong idea, which was actually the right idea within limits. I had plenty of limits.

During the intermission I saw Mrs. Fontana with a well-groomed man who might be her husband, the one who puts out the fires she starts. Saturday night at the theater meant little to Mrs. Fontana's grooming routine. She was wearing a sparkling pin that highlighted the disarray of her wrinkled dress.

"There's my English teacher," I said to Brett. "Want to say hello?"

"Sure. Maybe she'll give you a good mark for showing up at this play."

Brett took my hand and we tried to push our way through the crowd that was milling around. All I could think of was that he took my hand. Mrs. Fontana and her companion slipped from sight, but Brett kept holding my hand. Thanks, Mrs. Fontana, for bringing this about.

I surprised myself by getting engrossed in the second half of the play. It gripped me. The plot had gone from light to heavy, and even though I was familiar with it, it struck a chord in me. I was glad Brett had brought me. It was an intelligent kind of experience, a thinking one, you might say, and a shared one. It was different from seeing a grossed-out movie, something that socks you and socks you again. A movie like that can be shared, but it shares the screaming, juvenile part of you. Something about the play made me want to know everything about Brett from birth to this particular Saturday night. I postponed my kissing fantasies and thought about having a deep conversation with him. I hoped we'd go someplace to eat—any old grungy hangout would do—and talk and talk and talk.

Brett put his arm around me as we left the theater. I think Mrs. Fontana saw us from way in back. We chattered about the play as we headed back to the side street where Brett had parked his car.

We didn't see his car. There was an empty space where we thought he had parked it.

"I parked it on this street, didn't I?" he asked me. His arm wasn't around me anymore. He was scratching his head.

"I thought so. Didn't you park it in front of this imports store? I remember glancing at the embroidered shirts in the window."

"You're observant," he said. "I don't remember that."

"And didn't we pass the convenience store over there?"

"That I remember. Let's walk around and make sure. Maybe I parked on the other side of the theater."

"It's possible. It's not panic time yet."

We walked around the theater in all directions. The theater was the hub of our little universe of the disappearing car.

"I feel stupid doing this," Brett said finally. "I'm sure I parked it where we originally looked."

"I am too," I said. "But we have to be absolutely positive."

"Maybe I was in such provocative company I forgot where I was and I misplaced my car," Brett said. He put his arm around me again.

"Are you serious?"

"Serious."

Oh, how I wanted to find that car! And its front seat. The date had been perfect up until now. Except for finding out that Crystal Jameson had established a friendship beachhead. *That* I could live with, especially with Brett's arm around me. But where was Brett's car? Had someone from this poor, sad neighborhood decided that Brett's car could help pay for a way out? Or were some destructive joy riders spilling beer and dropping pizza crusts over my beautiful front seat? Were they in Nevada by now?

"Whose car is it?" I asked Brett finally. "Yours, your parents'?"

"My parents'. But it was on its way to becoming mine. They were planning to buy a new one and turn this over to me. But right now it's our one and only family car."

"Oh, dear."

The Palm Canyon Police Department moved in on our date. We had to call them. We couldn't find the car anywhere. Officers Caesar and Carter arrived about half an hour after Brett phoned them from the theater manager's office. Brett got a chance to know me better and I got a chance to know him better as we answered sharp questions from the police officers who were alternately sympathetic and weary.

"This is supposed to happen in New York City, not Palm Canyon," Brett informed them.

"No kidding. Tell me about it," Officer Caesar said. "No crime in the Sunbelt. Good to know, son. You're not a fan of crime statistics, I gather."

"Only this statistic," I said as politely as possible. "His car must have been stolen."

"Excellent, astute conclusion, young lady," Officer Carter said.

They were a pair. Officer Carter looked trim and stylish in her uniform, and Officer Caesar looked too small for his, as if he had just lost a lot of weight. They were partners, obviously.

Officer Caesar asked, "You didn't happen to leave your keys in the ignition, did you, son?"

Brett triumphantly brought forth his jingling keys from his pocket. Some triumph. There was no car to put a key into.

"Okay, I'll dispense with the lecture. That is, if you left your car doors locked and your windows up, and nothing tempting in full view on the seats."

"The only tempting thing left the car with me," Brett said.

I wished he hadn't gone that far. The remark was too flip, almost crass, and Officer Carter looked at us as if we were the kind of teenagers who make a car our home.

The officers didn't offer us a ride home. We could have asked, but arriving at my house in a police car didn't appeal to me. Brett told them we'd take a taxi or get a ride with a friend or family.

The officers left. My date with Brett was now really official. It was part of a police report. He apologized to me, but there was nothing to apologize for. I told him I was sure the police would find his car soon. It was a weak statement, coming from me. He would have preferred to hear it from the Caesar-Carter team, who promised nothing but an attempt to track down the car.

Dad was good-natured about driving us home. First he left Brett off. Was I supposed to walk Brett to his door? I didn't think so. Brett and I exchanged quips about what an interesting evening it had been, as he left the car. I didn't envy Brett having to tell his parents what had happened. I felt sad, very sad, to have our wonderful romantic evening turn into something else.

Dad and I went home. There was more than one robbery that evening. I was robbed of what might have been the best part of my date with Brett. Who had done this to me? To Brett? We might never find out. I knew that Crystal Jameson of the mean, ambitious eyes hadn't stolen Brett's car. But if it's possible to will a car to be stolen, she was guilty. Her Saturday date with Brett had a beginning and a middle and an end. Mine had a beginning and a middle and a larceny.

10

A few uneventful days went by. No cars belonging to anyone I knew were stolen. No cars belonging to anyone I knew were found. The girl from my English class who had passed by and said hi to me once on the way home from school did it again. In school I met a few more kids by name and I was beginning to get a feeling of settling in.

I ate my lunch outside because I wasn't ready to face Elissa at lunch or the sorority at lunch or anyone else at lunch. I needed a few days off. I saw Brett a couple of times in the halls. Once we were both in a hurry and once he stopped to tell me that the police had a lead on his car but nothing substantial. He didn't mention going out on a date again. Maybe his car and a date were tied together in his mind. Without a car he simply couldn't date. Maybe. Crystal Jameson gave me a huge hello one day. I wondered if she was getting together with Brett as a friend, suggesting carless activities, without the protocol or whatever it was of actually having to be picked up in a car for a date. Not a bad idea. I could do that too. Why not? Couldn't I suggest that Brett and I get together for studying or a walk or something? I guess, car or not, I was waiting for him to make the next move.

Elissa caught up with me on Wednesday on the way home from school.

"Hey, I've been missing you," she said. "What gives at lunch?"

"I've been bringing my lunch and eating outside. Just for a few days."

"Couldn't take the heat in the cafeteria so you opted for the heat outside?"

"Exactly what does that mean?"

"I saw you sitting at the sorority table last Friday. What were you doing there? Keeping the sorority seat warm?"

"The girls *invited* me," I said. It was a retort rather than an answer, but Elissa seemed to be taunting me.

"So where were they that they put you in quarantine and allowed you to stay there all by your lonesome?"

"They had a meeting outside. They were late getting to the cafeteria. By the time they got there, I was gone."

"You looked like a big shot sitting there. And a little shot, too."

"Let's just forget it," I said.

"Okay. Their excuse was probably legitimate, if it's any consolation. They've been having a bunch of minimeetings. The word's around that they're going to ask Crystal Jameson to fill one of their two vacancies."

"Oh?"

"Yeah, too bad. I hate to see someone like her get what she wants. I observe her, you know, and I hear things too. I know that when Crystal Jameson moved to town, her first major decision after choosing blood red for the color of her bedroom walls was to try to worm her way into Chi Kappa Sorority. And now her next major decision is . . ."

"Is what?"

"To steal Kim Adler's boyfriend."

"What?"

"Oh, c'mon. You've already translated her eyes."

I stopped walking. "I don't have a boyfriend, Elissa. If you're referring to Brett, we've only been out once."

"Oh, but he likes you, dear Kim. He likes you plenty. I can see it. So can Crystal. And she's got a good fifty-fifty chance of luring him away. I'm just glad she's not after . . ."

"After who?"

"Skip it."

Elissa meant Eric. But he wasn't Elissa's boyfriend. Had he ever, even once, asked her out? I wished she'd open up to me about him.

I started to walk again, which was a good idea because Elissa hadn't stopped, just slowed down slightly. When she said "Skip it" to me she had to almost yell it. When I got beside her I said, "I refuse to lock horns with any girl over a boy. Brett is intelligent enough to know his own mind, his own heart, or whatever influences him."

"That's a nice, empty, noble thought," Elissa said. "Keep that thought. It might be all you're left with."

Elissa was either vehemently trying to help me or was feeling irritated with me. She was agitated for sure. Our friendship had become . . . scratchy. My Friday residency at Buckingham Palace probably got under her skin. She didn't invite me to go to her house. I didn't want to go anyway. I had plenty of homework.

My mother was out on the golf course when I got home. I found a piece of mail on my bed. Mom always left my mail on my bed. It had started with an invitation to a birthday party when I was three. I couldn't read the invitation, but it was still mine. It was written by the mother of another three-year-old.

Now I hoped the envelope on my bed contained a letter from one of my New York friends. No one had written to me yet. Only Sidney Megovitch had been in touch. Sidney Megovitch! He would be calling "early evening" as we had arranged. And I hadn't even discussed his Thanksgiving visit with my parents. Brett and his car had more immediacy. To be honest with myself, almost anything had more immediacy. I had a Palm Canyon life that I wanted to concentrate on.

I picked up the envelope from my bed. There was a return address on it, but no return name. It was a Palm Canyon address. The envelope was a pale lavender kind of tan —the stationery of a girl or a liberated boy. Whoever had addressed it had studied calligraphy. Very ornate.

I tore open the envelope. There was an invitation inside, written by the same hand that had done the envelope:

> *Dear Kim,*
> *It is with great pleasure that we, the members of Chi Kappa Sorority, invite you to become a member of our group. Our next meeting is at the home of Selena Vonder, 8801 East Caligula Place, at which time we look forward to welcoming you into our membership as a sister. Please respond by calling Selena at the number printed below.*
> *Sororily yours,*
> *Rona Dunne, President*

"I'm in! *In!*" I screamed to the room. "They want me!" Everything would fall into place now. Brett, Palm Canyon, everything. It was all mine. I was a newcomer and it was all mine. I had no idea I would feel this way. The idea of becoming a member of Chi Kappa had been so remote that it had seemed beyond the perimeters of my life. If the sorority hadn't invited me to become a member, I would have said "Who cares?" and I would have meant it. But the reality of being asked to join opened up all my dreams of really belonging in Palm Canyon. Part of that sorority table in the cafeteria would truly be mine for the remainder of my high school career. Even if I sat alone there from time to time, I wouldn't care. Because everyone would know I belonged.

I didn't kiss the invitation. But I sat holding it, hoping that my mother would be home soon. She would be thrilled. Who else could I tell? My father. But he wasn't crazy about groups. Brett? He would be impressed, wouldn't he? But wait. Wouldn't it be better if the news reached him roundabout? It would be news *about* me, but not *from* me. Cool. Nice and cool. None of this juvenile eager-beaver stuff.

I remembered Elissa. My feeling of joy drained away. But not for long. Maybe I could get Elissa into the sorority. But she was a mystery. Did she want to get in? She acted like she didn't and yet she had played up to Tracy McVane when we were at the sorority table. If she didn't want to get in, she would have no right to resent my becoming a member. She must have been off base thinking that Crystal Jameson was a candidate. If Crystal was a candidate she would have full-blasted the news immediately. Still, Crystal might only now be getting an invitation like mine. I knew there were two vacancies. If Crystal got invited it would be a double blow for Elissa. Her friend and her enemy joined in the ranks of Chi Kappa.

Eating lunch outside tomorrow seemed like an increasingly smart idea. Avoid everyone until all precincts have been heard from.

My parents happened to arrive home at almost the same moment. I had calmed down by then. I decided to break my news while we were sitting around the supper table. I said, "Guess who's been invited to become a member of Chi Kappa Sorority?"

My mother's face exploded in triumph. My father started to eat his soup. "Well, Kim," he said, "you can always quit if you don't like it."

"Harris!" My mother was horrified.

"Dad, thanks for your enthusiasm. Nobody quits the sorority."

"That sounds ominous. So you're stuck with

this group for your entire junior and senior years. You escape when you graduate?"

"Not stuck. Honored. Look, it's hard enough to get in. They picked me."

"Harris, you might try congratulating your daughter instead of tearing the sorority apart. It's just a social club, dear."

"Oh, well, why didn't you say so? This club is exclusive, shallow, and meaningless. It doesn't stand for anything. It's full of the good, uncomplicated freewheeling cheer of noncommitment. Excellent. You can't always find all that under one roof. I strongly approve."

"Don't be cute, Harris."

"I'm not cute. I'm adorable. Does the sorority need a mascot?"

"I'll ask," I said. I was grinning. I couldn't be mad at my father. He believed what he believed.

"You won't ask," my father said. "You'll sit quiet as a mouse at the first meeting, properly obsequious and awed by your surroundings."

Was my father right? I was scared of the first meeting. I might be the only newcomer, the novice, the odd one. But it would be worth it.

Kim Adler, member, Chi Kappa Sorority.

11

Sidney Megovitch's phone call was my dessert, shared with a peach cobbler. I was prepared for the peach cobbler. I was with Mom at the supermarket when she bought the peaches for it. But Sidney had slipped my mind. Off and on I had remembered his Thanksgiving request, but it was never at a time when I could discuss it with my parents or really think it through myself. Everything else going on in my life had preempted Sidney. Sidney was not a prime-time priority.

I cheerfully answered the phone when it rang. I was in high spirits. I didn't care who was on the other end of the line. The sorority girl was taking her first phone call.

But it was a bit of a shocker to hear Sidney's voice. He was on time. We did have a telephone appointment. But I was totally ill-prepared for it. What could I do? How would it sound to say, "Excuse me, Sidney, while I break the news to my parents about your proposed Thanksgiving visit and then discuss it with them while your long-distance charges go zooming upwards"?

I had answered the call at the kitchen phone. Sidney said, "Hi, Kim." I replied, "Hi,

Sidney." So far, perfection. You couldn't want a better telephone meeting of the minds.

Then Sidney said, "Are things set for my visit?"

I said, "Yes."

He said, "Great."

I said nothing.

He said, "I'll call you again and tell you when my plane arrives. I can take a taxi from the airport unless you want to meet me."

I said, "We'll see what's best."

He said "Great" again.

Then he said, "I'm counting the days to Thanksgiving."

I said, "I think I'll be doing that, too, Sidney."

"I love you, Kim," he said. "Bye."

"Bye, Sidney."

Mom has an expression: "No muss, no fuss, no bother." That perfectly fit my conversation with Sidney. It had been no problem really. I just went along with Sidney's plans. A snap. At some point in time, preferably never, I would have to come to grips with what I had done, or hadn't done. I would have to break the news to my parents that Sidney Megovitch was flying across the country to spend Thanksgiving with us. I had no idea how they wanted to spend this first Thanksgiving in Palm Canyon. For all I knew, they might get an invitation to somebody's house.

"Who was that on the phone?" Mom called from the dining room.

"A solicitor."

"What is it now? Free dancing lessons? Baby photographs? An all-expenses-paid vacation trip?"

"Sort of the last."

"What's the hitch? What do they want from us?"

"Just a little love."

"Naturally. Come finish your peach cobbler, Kim."

"In a minute."

I picked up the receiver again. I should call Sidney back. Forget it. Worry about it tomorrow. Next week.

I called Selena Vonder.

She answered the phone. My voice trembled slightly. I didn't know Selena. I wished I had been directed to call Tracy or one of the flower twins or even Rona.

"Hi," I said. "This is Kim Adler."

I waited for an outpouring of congratulations.

"Who?"

"Kim Adler."

"Oh, yes, yes. Sorry. I didn't expect you to call so soon."

My call was as welcome as Sidney's.

"The card, the invitation, said to phone you."

"Right, of course."

"Well, I'm just calling to accept. I didn't want to keep you waiting." I giggled slightly. "I see you weren't exactly waiting, but anyway, thanks. I'm really happy to be invited to become a sorority sister."

"Fabulous. We're all so pleased, Kim. We'll be expecting you at our next meeting. The time and date are at the bottom of your invitation. Oh, and please don't say anything to anyone else until you've been sworn in as a member."

"Sworn in?"

"Yes. At the meeting. Until then we won't be asking you to sit with us or anything. It's just to keep the secret a secret."

"I'm not supposed to tell anyone?"

"I'm sure you'll want to tell your parents if you haven't already. But do ask them not to spread the word around."

I felt relieved. I *couldn't* tell Elissa just yet. This was much easier for me than trying to find the right time to break the news. Perhaps I could soften it, talk up the sorority, somehow get Elissa to accept my new position before she actually knew what it was.

12

There was no high drama in the cafeteria. I resumed eating there. Elissa joined me most of the time, but occasionally she'd just wave to me and go sit at another table. It was possible that I had been cramping *her* style, that she had felt obliged to sit with me when she really wanted to spread herself around. The sorority girls acknowledged me with big smiles whenever we saw one another. By now I was getting to recognize more sorority faces.

One day Crystal Jameson sat herself down across from me. Two other girls were already sitting at my table. I didn't know them, and they didn't introduce themselves, but they said "Hi" in a friendly way when they joined me.

Crystal placed her tray on the table delicately, sort of sliding it toward the other trays that were already there, trying to make a neat, symmetrical pattern of trays. Ridiculous. But typical for a girl who made a career out of maneuvering.

"What's new?" Crystal said to me like she was an old friend. She started to drink the half pint of milk that came with her lunch.

"Everything and nothing," I answered.

"My father's shirt didn't fit him, would you believe it?"

She was launching the conversation with her father's shirt. She had something to tell me about Brett.

"What shirt is that?" I asked innocently.

"The shirt that Brett helped me pick out."

"Too bad."

"Only temporarily. Brett was nice enough to go back and help me pick out another shirt. This time it really fit."

She wasn't going to get a reaction out of me. She was telling me she'd been with Brett twice. I let it slide by.

"Where do you shop?" I asked.

I was thinking transportation. Brett didn't have a car. How did they get to wherever they went?

"Palm Canyon Mall. They have the best selection."

"Brett doesn't have a car," I said. I hadn't meant to say that. And of course she already knew.

"I don't mind taking buses. It's not forever anyway. I'm getting my driver's learner permit."

She didn't mind taking buses! She probably dragged Brett onto the bus. Brett, I decided on the spot, was your basic bus hater. When he thought of me, he thought of cars with plush front seats. That was it. He would never take me on a date by bus.

The two girls at our table had been half listening to our conversation. One of them asked, "Are you talking about Brett Fox? What a hunk. I'd take a bus with him anytime, anywhere."

The other girl laughed and said, "I'd stand at a bus stop under a blazing sun with him until the vultures came to pick our bones."

Crystal smiled at the girls and kept sipping her milk. Brett was catching on with the girls at Palm Canyon High. I knew it would happen. And face it, he knew he had caught on with Crystal. He was smart enough to realize that she wasn't just interested in him as a shirt model or a pal. I was making excuses to myself about the bus, about the car. Worthless empty excuses. But I wasn't going to allow myself to get depressed. It was too soon to give up on Brett. I had a father, just like Crystal had, who might appreciate a new shirt. Forget that one. Crystal had used it up, and my father was barely five nine, anyway.

I ate my lunch calmly, as if I hadn't gotten considerably wiser in the past few minutes. What I would do about my new wisdom, I didn't know. I had other problems to work out. The sorority meeting was coming up. I had dropped a few small comments about the

sorority girls to Elissa. "They're not so bad."
"We should judge them as individuals, not as a
group. My dad says that groups bring out the
worst in people."

"What if groups bring out the best?" Elissa
said. "What if each sorority girl is even worse
all by herself?"

Elissa was not going to be converted. She
had some friends, I noticed that. Not a lot, but
she wasn't desperate. Except possibly about
Eric. He hadn't joined us at lunch again. I
didn't see them together anywhere. It could
be a hopeless situation that Elissa would have
to learn to accept. Unless she lost weight.
That could make a difference. Or no difference at all. But she wasn't trying.

I was starting to count the days until the
sorority meeting. "Counting the days" was an
expression I had last heard coming from the
lips of Sidney Megovitch. Now *that* was a
problem I could do something about. I was
going to cancel Sidney. Not as a person, but as
a visitor. It would be insane to let him visit us
for Thanksgiving. Let his parents take Sidney
to Palm Springs with them.

I would definitely take care of the Sidney
situation *after* the sorority meeting. It would
be sticky, and I didn't want to spoil the pure
happiness I felt every time I thought of the
meeting. My father offered to drive me over

to Selena Vonder's house. He had clammed
up about the sorority. He was trying to act
positive. Mom didn't have to try. She was
walking on air. Hot air I'm afraid. She made
several long-distance calls to her friends and
surviving relatives in New York telling them
that an absolutely marvelous, top, prestigious,
you-name-it sorority had begged me to become a member.

Mom insisted that I wear something new to
the meeting. She wasn't a fan of Thoreau's.

13

They were all sitting around the living room of Selena Vonder's house, waiting for me. Altogether, as a group, they looked civilized, groomed, pruned in a way, like trees shorn of unwanted branches. I had heard that last year they were sloppy and meticulously unkempt. But that had gone out of style over the summer. And the sorority was always in style. Except perhaps for Tracy McVane, who had found a rainbow and was exhibiting it, color by color, strand by strand, in her hair.

I was late. Why was I late? Because I was nervous, and nervous can make you too early or it can make you late. It throws off your timing.

There were eight of them, the sorority sisters, and they all smiled at me at the same time. Daisy Baron, the twin who tried less hard, had a sincere and open smile. Almost the smile of a friend. There were two other pleasant, agreeable smiles, one funhouse-mirror smile, distorted and hiding whatever was behind it, and three bland but slightly arrogant smiles. Then there was the president's smile. Rona Dunne was not only the most popular girl at Palm Canyon High, she was the owner of the-most-popular smile. It was the princess of smiles.

I stood there. There were no empty seats. A couple of the girls were sitting on the floor.

"Hi, Kim," Rona said. "Let me introduce you around. We all know who you are, of course, but just for the record, girls, this is Kim Adler."

I stood there, Exhibit A. I didn't want to be *known* by them. It didn't feel comfortable to be known by girls you hardly knew. Half of the girls were total strangers, although I remembered seeing most of them around school. Carrie Reis, the cheerleader. She had a chiseled profile and a lavender car. Elissa had told me about the car. Elissa had also told me about Allie Grendler. Her family was the richest in town, but Allie always wore clothes that made a moral statement. They were handmade by a poverty-stricken tribe somewhere in South America, and Allie wore their clothes as an announcement of their plight. There was another girl, sitting quietly, passively. I had never seen her.

Rona said, "Kim, you know Tracy of course. And Daisy and Tulip. Selena, our hostess. Carrie Reis, the world's best cheerleader. Allie Grendler, our conscience, and Melanie Deborah Kane. But please don't call her Mel or Melanie. It's Melanie Deborah."

"I'm a survivor," Melanie Deborah volunteered.

Was that connected to her name or something else in her life or was this her favorite catch phrase? Was I facing two years of "I'm a survivor"? I had left "It just blows me away" back in New York, the favorite expression of seven-year-old Shannon Megovitch.

I said "Hi" and kind of looked around the room so that everyone would know they were included. Then I started to sit down next to Melanie Deborah.

"Uh-uh," Rona said quickly. "Don't sit down, Kim. You have to be sworn in first. We can't allow outsiders to be privy to what goes on at our meetings, and you're an outsider until you're sworn in. We used to have initiation ceremonies, but we got complaints from parents and the school administration, so that's all gone bye-bye. Now, who has the Bible?"

"I do." Carrie Reis held up a book and a slip of paper. "I have the oath too. Everyone please notice that this is my first act as your new secretary."

Someone giggled.

A Bible! A swearing-in on a Bible. Wasn't this going too far? I said, "If you don't mind, this doesn't hit me quite right. The sorority is a social club and I think this is kind of heavy."

"We've all done it," Rona said.

Tracy held up her hand. "Correction. Five years ago somebody refused, and two years before that. I've researched."

Tracy, as editor of the school newspaper, had power. Power that the sorority respected. It overrode her neon-bright hair colorings, and almost every wild thing she might want to do. She was, simply stated, their resident brain, and quite possibly their only brain of any substance. I supposed that Tracy used her power wisely or unwisely according to her mood. She kept talking. "I say there are two precedents for not swearing on the Bible and we go with that."

I was happy to go with that.

"Hear! Hear! Tracy's got the word!" Tulip Baron, sitting on a love seat with her twin Daisy, raised her hand. Tulip raising her hand was the same as Daisy and Tulip raising their hands. Everyone seemed to think of them as one unit. Therefore, there were two votes to go along with Tracy.

Rona tapped on the piano bench where she was sitting. "Let's get on with this. Forget the Bible. Kim, just repeat after me: *I promise to uphold the high ideals of Chi Kappa Sorority wherever I am and forever. I will never under any circumstances divulge to outsiders what I see or hear at Chi Kappa meetings.*"

Rona made the words sound inspiring, majestic. I repeated them in a flat little voice. It was embarrassing, like reciting the Pledge of Allegiance all by myself in front of people and hoping not to flub a word.

There was a small round of applause. Then everyone rose up and kissed me. "Welcome, sister member of Chi Kappa."

I had been transformed into a new person. I could now sit down on the floor.

Rona tapped the piano bench again. "Girls, we have one crucial matter to discuss tonight."

"Yeah, how much the dues will be this year." Selena Vonder laughed. "Look, I'm the treasurer and I still don't know how much to hit everyone up for." Selena held out her hands, ten fuchsia flags of nails waving.

Is it awful to think bad thoughts about someone whose home you're a guest in? I was in Selena's house. This was the setting for my success. I had become a sorority sister right here on Vonder property. I tried to remember what Elissa had once said about Selena. That she had the biggest, loudest mouth in town. That it was a repository of malice, a garbage dump of gossip. Elissa said that Selena had blackmailed her way into the sorority. If so, score one for the sorority. They wouldn't let in anyone of Selena's caliber except under duress. Still, I didn't know Selena, and I had to make my own judgments. I hoped I wouldn't slip and call her Sleazena the way Elissa did.

Rona looked impatient. "Selena, the dues are the same as last year. I'm talking about choosing our tenth member. The rules of the sorority state that we must always be ten in number. There's a grace period during which we select our new members after former members leave. But we've let this period drag on for too long. We were fortunate in being able to make a decision about Kim to take the place of one of our graduated seniors. But tonight we have to select our tenth member. I'm open to suggestions."

"Crystal Jameson," said Melanie Deborah Kane.

I froze. But I kept quiet.

Rona frowned. "She seems a likely choice, but somehow she doesn't seem right for us."

This was getting interesting.

"What does that mean, Rona?" Tracy twirled an orangy lock of hair around a finger.

"Crystal Jameson is—how do I put it—*courting* us. She's like a suitor. She wants in. I resent it."

"Some girls have to try harder than you, Rona," Tulip said. "They have to worm and wiggle their way into popularity."

Tracy spoke up. "No, Rona's right. I haven't said anything because I wanted to get some other reactions first."

"Hold on," said Rona. "I'm not disqualifying Crystal. I'm just saying that she doesn't seem right for us. But perhaps if we let her in she'll settle down. She might make a good sister if we give her a chance. But let's hear some other suggestions."

Rona was asking, she definitely was.

"Elissa Hanes," I said in a firm voice.

"Elissa Hanes? She's fat!" Selena Vonder's witch voice dominated the room. I was in a coven.

"Now just a minute," I said. "That's mean."

Rona looked me straight in the eye. "You've been a member for ten minutes, dear. We like our opinions seasoned around here. You know, not *nouveau* opinions."

I had planned to sit still, watch, and listen, the proper behavior of a newcomer to a group. But Rona was asking for nominations. And now the word fat had jolted me.

Rona's voice softened. "Elissa Hanes is a friend of yours, isn't she, Kim? She happens to be a very smart girl." Rona paused. Then she said, "Girls, Elissa is really bright."

Allie Grendler smoothed her moral statement of a dress. She frowned. "I personally like Elissa Hanes. But I'd have to think—really think—about whether I'd want her in the sorority. Let's all picture her sitting here in this room with all of us."

Tracy McVane was muttering. "Elissa's smart. I could use some company in that area."

Allie pouted. "Don't be fresh, Tracy. Being the editor of the paper doesn't make you a genius or anything."

Rona said, "Surely the membership can come up with more than two names. Keep in mind that we are, under some circumstances, even willing to consider freshmen."

"How about Fiona Kasselman?" Selena asked.

"Who?" Daisy Baron looked puzzled.

"Fiona Kasselman. She's a freshman."

"Does anyone know Fiona Kasselman except Selena?" Rona asked.

"I don't know her," Selena said. "I had this idea that it might be fun to sort of pluck an ordinary freshman from the crowd and see if we can mold her into something special."

"Forget it," Melanie Deborah said. "I think Crystal Jameson is special already. She's a survivor, you know."

"How's that?" asked Tracy.

Melanie Deborah shrugged.

"I think she's a predator," Selena said. "I admire her."

"Elissa Hanes has a head," Tracy said.

"And a body, too," Selena said, laughing. "Let's not forget that."

"Selena, that's enough," Rona said. "We've discussed Elissa in the past. She has unique qualities, we've all agreed. Now, ask yourself are those unique qualities for Chi Kappa? We seem to have settled on two candidates, and I want all of you to concentrate on this most important decision. Kim, you'll be voting too. We vote by secret ballot, and we don't require one hundred percent approval for a candidate. A yes vote of six members will win membership for a girl. You can't vote for both candidates, but you can abstain from voting for either one. Is that clear?"

We all nodded.

"Good," Rona said. "I'm going to hand out slips of paper. Please write the name Crystal Jameson or Elissa Hanes on your slip of paper. Remember, do not write both names. If you wish, you can leave your paper blank. If neither girl gets the minimum six votes, we'll have to start all over again with other names. Don't rush. *Think!* This is important. We have an entire school to choose from."

I wished I could have written the name Elissa Hanes six times. Not only did I want Elissa in the sorority, I *needed* her. Rona Dunne might be the most popular girl in school but tonight she had taken on the aura of the head of a small-time terrorist group. A couple of the girls weren't bad. I was beginning to like Tracy. Daisy Baron had potential. Melanie Deborah was too busy being a survivor to clue me in on anything else about her. Rona herself was trying to be fair but she had an unfair way of going about it. All in all, though, coven had not been an inaccurate way to describe this collection of girls.

I wrote the name Elissa Hanes boldly, passed in my paper, and waited for Rona to announce the name of the new member, if there was one.

In three feverishly scribbled minutes Crystal Jameson was voted in as the tenth member of Chi Kappa Sorority.

14

The meeting went on.

Rona said, "Crystal Jameson will be invited to our next meeting. And now Allie will fill us in on our first social event of the season. Allie, a progress report please."

Allie took some papers from her pocket-book, which was hanging by its strap over the back of her chair. She glanced down at the papers. Then she raised her eyes. "Well, our first social event of the season is . . . in place! We have a room at the Palm Canyon Country Club for our dance, and for those of you who can spring for a limo—if you want to take your guys in style—my parents got us a deal on that too. I'd like to hear a round of applause for my parents, who helped arrange this."

A couple of the girls whistled. I didn't know what Allie was talking about. It all sounded kind of rich. What was I getting myself into?

Rona asked a cool, president-type question: "What kind of money are we talking about, Allie?"

"Not to worry," Allie said. She shuffled her papers like TV newscasters do when they don't have anything else to do. "My dad got one of his accountants to figure everything

out. The room, the band, a buffet dinner—
everything at a big discount, you understand,
thanks to my parents' pull—thirty couples
and we break even. Anything over that is
profit. Limos, for those who want them, are in
the package but they're extra. So there'll be
ten couples from the sorority—I mean we're
all going, you better believe it—and then we
open it up to the public and pull in twenty
more couples, and we're all set. And I think
we'll do better than that and make a profit.
The room holds well over one hundred people."

"What if we don't get those twenty couples?" Tracy asked. "We could be in the hole."

"Trust me," Allie said. "This'll be a charity
function. See, that's how we'll advertise it.
Any profit we make, we'll give a certain per-
centage to charity. I've got the charity." Allie
smoothed her dress again.

"How much to charity?" Tracy asked.

Allie shrugged. "Probably ten percent, but
that's not anybody's business but the sorority's. The big thing is that we promote this as a
charity event."

"Ten percent?" Tracy looked disturbed.
"And we keep ninety percent for ourselves?
Not too charitable."

I agreed with Tracy. I spoke up. "Not too
charitable," I repeated. Rona stared me

down. *"Nouveau,* Kim, *nouveau."* I let it pass. Maybe I was too new.

"Tracy," Selena said, ignoring me, "that's ten percent more than the charity would have received."

"I'm not following this," Melanie Deborah said. "You lost me somewhere."

I was lost too. But in a different way. I had missed the earlier meetings of the sorority so I had catching up to do. But I did pick up on "if you want to take your guys in style" and I knew the sorority was having a girls-invite-the-boys dance. I could invite Brett! If the other girls were inviting boys, that made it okay for me to invite Brett.

Rona looked perplexed. "There's something missing here, Allie. You haven't told us how much each of us will have to pay. Just a crucial minor item. What did your father's accountant compute?"

Allie hesitated. "Figuring thirty couples attend, okay?"

Rona sighed. "Go ahead."

"Okay, then. More than ten dollars per couple, but less than one hundred."

"Less than one hundred!" Selena's voice shrieked. This time, it seemed to me, it had a legitimate reason to shriek.

Melanie Deborah repeated, "Less than one hundred. I'll never survive *that!"*

"Neither will the rest of us, Melanie Deborah," Rona said. "Stop the jesting, Allie, and pin it down. What did your meticulous little accountant with his pursed lips and furrowed brow and chewed-off pencil . . ."

"He doesn't have a chewed-off pencil," Allie said. "He's got a computer."

I wasn't listening anymore. I could see myself at the Palm Canyon Country Club in a beautiful dress with beautiful music in the background and I'd be dancing with Brett and laughing with Brett and being romantic with Brett. And what was this about a limo? Since Brett didn't have a car, I'd take him in a limo! I'd never have enough guts to do something as fabulous as this on my own, but with the sorority behind me, I could do anything. I was glad I was a member. I tried not to think about Elissa. I tried not to think about all the money this was going to cost.

All the girls seemed to be talking at once. They forgot about me. They forgot that all of this was news to me. When was this dance taking place, anyway?

Finally I picked up more information. Selena's voice shrilled across the room. "I hope this dance won't turn out to be a turkey. We sure have the right weekend for it."

Turkey? Thanksgiving! It had to be. The
dance was on Thanksgiving weekend.
I had two phone calls to make. One to Brett
Fox and one to Sidney Megovitch.

15

Refreshments were served. Elegant minia-ture frosted pastries, croissants, soft drinks, and tea. The best part of the meeting. The Baron twins gave me a ride home. Daisy had offered. There was something appealing about her that was canceled out by the prox-imity of her sister. Daisy was shortchanged by being part of a unit.

By the time I got home it was too late to telephone anybody. My parents were en-grossed in a TV show so I went to my room. I found an envelope on my bed. Not another invitation! The front of the envelope had KIM printed on it. There was a greeting card in-side. It had a drawing of an animal in a forest. The animal was looking at a tree. A CON-GRATULATIONS! sign was hanging from a branch. There was a parade of joyous elves around the tree.

The card, signed with x's, was from my mother. I was sure she had picked it out with great care. My father dreamed up ideas for a living; my mother went out and bought other people's ideas. Mom was short on originality. She bought other people's sentiments on greeting cards, mugs, T-shirts. Sentiments paid for had authority. My father's, on the other hand, were homemade. Dad didn't mind. He thought it was funny.

I stared at the card and felt tense. Maybe paid-for sentiments did have authority. My membership in Chi Kappa was a real happening, like a wedding or a graduation. Tomorrow I would have to tell Elissa that I was a member of the sorority. The thought of that killed me. I would not tell her that I proposed her name for membership and she had been rejected. Tomorrow I would also ask Brett, in person, to go to the Thanksgiving dance with me. And after school I would call Sidney and tell him that he couldn't come to visit me. Maybe by tomorrow night I could have all of that behind me and I could relax again.

I wondered how fast the word would spread about my getting into Chi Kappa. Would anyone come up and congratulate me? Maybe not. There was something unapproachable about the sorority, and now I had become part of the unapproachableness. Still, maybe Brett would be impressed. Of course he'd be impressed!

The next day on the way to school I found out how fast the word had spread. Someone called "Kim!" I turned around. It was Elissa.

She looked puffy and tense. Maybe it was my imagination. We started to walk together.

Her clumsy walk had disappeared. She was a member of the military. "Congratulations on becoming a member of the hierarchy," she said.

She was angry.

No point in being coy. "How did you find out so soon? Never mind, I was going to tell you today."

"Why didn't you tell me last week? You knew it was going to happen."

"I wasn't supposed to tell in advance. And anyway, it's such a hard thing to do. I was afraid it would hurt our friendship. It won't, will it, Elissa? I mean you don't care about the sorority, do you?"

She didn't answer me directly. She didn't say yes. She didn't say no. She said, "They've been, shall we say, considering *me* for membership, off and on. I hear. I know. They're interested in me because I've got the reputation of being the smartest girl in school, and I guess I've got the marks to prove it too. But then there's the little matter of my weight. It's been fluctuating up and down, mostly up. If the sorority had an opening last year when I went on my crash diet and lost fifteen pounds, I'd probably be a member today."

She knew. How did she know? Maybe Tracy had told her, or hinted. What if Elissa found out that she was rejected again last night?

She had more to say. "The sorority needs a brain balance. Popularity they've got. Looks they've got. They've got enough surface stuff to cover the earth. But they're short on brains. They've got Tracy. She'll go on to Princeton, I bet. Now they've got you. So there's one opening left. Or is it closed? You're public knowledge now. You've been sworn in. But the tenth member, it's Crystal Jameson, isn't it? She's thinner than me. In her own way, she's a very hungry girl too. Know what I mean?"

"Elissa, maybe you wouldn't like the sorority after you got in."

"Of course I wouldn't. I don't like it now."

"So if you just want to join something, why not something nice like the Stamp Club?"

"I don't do stamps."

"How about the French Club? I know you speak French. Or an animal club. How about the Save-the . . . the . . ."

"Whales? Buffaloes? Eagles? I might be interested in doing something for the coyotes here, which brings me right back to the sorority."

"I don't understand, Elissa. *Why* the sorority?"

Elissa's plump face spread out in accordian

pleats of fat as she grinned. "Because I want to *quit!* Nobody has ever quit, don't you see? I'd be the first one. I'd be a symbol. I'd be fighting back for every blemished entity that ever existed. For every person or thing that has ever been rejected anywhere for any reason. Every scruffy dog passed by in the pound, every dented car snubbed by purchasers, every bruised banana in the supermarket, every bald head, every pimple, every scar, and every pound of excessive weight."

I reached over and hugged Elissa. "Elissa, you're wonderful. Too wonderful to belong to that sorority for even five minutes."

"So why are you in it?" she asked.

She pushed me away. She had said her piece. She was finished with me. Finished. She walked off.

Why had I joined Chi Kappa? They had rejected Elissa because she was fat. Oh, I should have grabbed and eaten every one of those fancy pastries they served after the meeting. And that would be just the beginning. I should gain thirty pounds, fifty pounds, eighty pounds, and the sorority will be stuck with ultra fat Kim Adler for two miserable years. I can sit around their lovely living rooms and take up the space of two members, and pat my ever-expanding body with great relish. But why stop there? I can bring further honor to the name of Chi Kappa. I can pick up a tube of lipstick in a store, hide it with a conspicuous flourish under my jacket, walk out of the store, and when I'm caught announce my name and affiliation with Chi Kappa Sorority. I can also take off my clothes in the middle of assembly at school and say that I represent Chi Kappa Sorority in its finest hour. Dream on, Kim. Fantasy bravery comes cheap.

Who knows what the girls of Chi Kappa really think about *me?* What had they said about me before they voted me in? Did they pull me apart? What kind of marks did I get on that quiz they gave me at their table that day? It was an entrance exam, I knew that now. And I had passed. But what if they really pulled me apart before putting me back together again and inviting me in. I didn't want to know.

16

My day got better. Brett was waiting for me at school before my first class. He must have checked up on where I'd be. He greeted me with "Hey, Kim, guess what vehicle was found by the Palm Canyon Police Department?"

"You got your car back?"

"In a manner of speaking. A few things were stripped from it—things that help the car to start, for example, and to keep going, for another example, and to stop, for another example."

"Oh, no!"

"It's not that bad. It's getting fixed. How about celebrating its recovery by going out with me just as soon as it's all back together?"

"I'd love it!"

I had been right. Brett didn't think of me as a bus person. Here was my chance to invite him to the sorority dance. I felt better about it now that he had invited me out again. But it would almost seem like an even exchange. He was asking me out. I was asking him out. I could wait until I was back in that wonderful front seat. Also I could hit up my parents for the money in the meantime. It wasn't going to be cheap going to that dance. What if my parents turned me down?

"When will your car be fixed?"

"It should be set by Saturday night. I'll talk to you later in the week, okay?"

"Great."

Apparently he hadn't heard about my getting into the sorority. Should I tell him right now? Would it sound like I was showing off? Let him hear it from someone else. If he doesn't, he'll find out soon enough when I invite him to the dance Saturday night.

Brett left to go to his first class. As he walked away I suddenly had regrets that I didn't invite him to the dance on the spot. The news of the dance was going to be publicized soon. Another girl might ask him. Crystal! No. The sorority girls were inviting their own dates first before opening up the dance to the public. This was the way it was done. And Crystal wasn't a member yet, not until the next meeting, which was at least a week away. Crystal had to be sworn in. The girls were sticklers on that.

I felt like a different person at school, but different in what way, I wasn't sure. Elissa totally ignored me at lunch. She didn't even wave. I sat at the sorority table, for the first time as a member. I had been locked out before. But now, as I looked around the cafeteria, I wondered if I was exclusive or simply locked *in*. The sorority table might not be Buckingham Palace. It might be the royal prison. There were three girls at the table with me. Tulip, Allie, and Carrie. They were as friendly as puppies to me. They chatted on and on about the Thanksgiving dance. They asked me if I knew who I'd be inviting. I said, "Could be," and that seemed to satisfy them.

The girl from my English class who always said hi to me congratulated me on becoming a member of Chi Kappa. She was with a couple of other girls who looked at me with just a bit of admiration.

The word was definitely spreading.

17

The walks home from school seemed to be getting hotter instead of cooler. Mom was in a swimsuit by the pool, waiting for me when I got home. We had had a nice breakfast together that morning while she grilled me about the sorority and I thanked her for her card. But now she looked annoyed.

"Kim," she said, "you got a phone call not five minutes ago. I had to scramble out of the pool. But that's not the point."

"Oh? Something wrong? It wasn't from one of my teachers, was it? I'm doing okay in school, honestly."

"Your telephone call, Kim, was not from one of your teachers. It was not from anyone in Palm Canyon. It was not from anyone in the state of Arizona. Your call was long-distance from Sidney Megovitch in New York informing me what airline he's taking for his Thanksgiving visit with us. His Thanksgiving *visit?* Naturally I knew nothing about it. It was very embarrassing to say the least. Explain, please."

I explained as best I could. I ended with "You know Sidney."

"I certainly do."

"I'm sorry, Mom," I said. "But I'm kind of glad it happened this way. I was going to call Sidney and tell him he couldn't visit us, and now you've done it for me. It softens the blow, coming from you instead of me. Did he take it hard?"

"Take it hard? I told him he could come. At first I didn't know what he was talking about, and I had to get my thoughts together. His mother is quite a nice person. Remember, she recommended that dentist we liked so much in New York? And we have that lovely guest suite downstairs, unused. Sidney's no problem. He's cute. Dad loves him. They can have one of their endless chess games."

"He's *coming?* You said okay?"

"Why not? But he's basically your guest, don't forget. I didn't know that you didn't want him. I thought you were fond of him in a big-sister way. And he's a friend from New York. New York! Doesn't that make you feel good?"

"Well, no. I'm busy that weekend. At least on Saturday night of the weekend. The sorority is having a big dance. I didn't mention it this morning because I've been trying to figure out how to hit you up for the money I'll need. It'll cost."

"Money for a sorority dance? You've got it. Dad and I will be happy to supply it."

"And Dad will play chess with Sidney the night of the dance, okay? The rest of the time I'll show him around, be his hostess or something."

"We can all do that, Kim. And we're planning to have Thanksgiving dinner here at home. Our first Thanksgiving in Palm Canyon."

I sat down in one of the lounge chairs by the pool. "Mom, this is *wonderful!* Thank you. I was getting frantic about Sidney. I was going to cancel him. This solves everything."

"Who are you going to the sorority dance with? Brett? What's the story with his car?"

"Yes, I'm inviting Brett. Taking him, actually. I'm asking him Saturday night when we're out on our next date. His car was found. It has some problems, but it's being fixed and we're going out in it. At least that's the plan. Speaking of cars, limos are available for the sorority dance, at a price. They come with a chauffeur. You get picked up and then you get driven to your date's house and he gets picked up. I don't know how much that costs yet."

Mom smiled. "Now that's a sorority with style. Dad and I will discuss the limo once you get a price. But with or without a limo, everything sounds so exciting. Are you happy?"

"Sure."

I was semihappy. No. Less than that. An awful feeling of sadness came over me whenever I thought about Elissa. And I was thinking about her more and more. My mother went back into the pool and I went to my room to start on my homework. I opened a book and thought about Elissa sitting down next to me that first day of school. I remembered her beckoning arm and how she got Brett to come over to our table. I remembered her saying that Brett and I could become the killer couple in school. I thought of all the remarks she had made about the sorority. And finally I knew what she really wanted. Elissa wanted her own kind of power. She wanted friends who might give it to her. That's why she latched onto the promising new kids at school. She wanted, within her own terms and her own territory, to be *in*. I couldn't blame her. That's what I wanted too.

What could I do for Elissa? I had tried to get her into the sorority and I failed. I believed what she said this morning, that she would quit if she got in. It was the ultimate power.

I felt helpless. Then I remembered something else about that first day of school. Actually I remembered someone else. Eric Day. Elissa had a thing for Eric. It had nothing to do with power or being in or out. It was a girl-boy thing. Elissa was far from being a passive person and yet I had never seen her do anything aggressive about Eric. She must care for him a lot to repress her natural self.

I closed my book and opened another. A telephone book. There were several Days listed in it. After two calls, I found Eric.

18

"Eric?"

"Yeah."

"Hi. This is Kim Adler."

"Oh, hi."

"Eric?"

"Yeah, this is Eric. My name hasn't changed from a second ago."

I was thankful for his sense of humor. That made things easier.

"Eric, I've become a member of Chi Kappa Sorority."

"No kidding. Say that's great. They've kind of got their noses in the air sometimes, but you'll turn them around."

"Thanks. Eric?"

"You're gonna wear out my name from overuse."

"Sorry."

"That's okay. There's nothing as sweet as the sound of my own name. Wait, strike that. I sound like a member of the sorority."

"This phone call has something to do with the sorority. We're having a dance on Thanksgiving weekend. That Saturday night. It's all very hush-hush right now until we go public. Which will be soon."

"Yeah, I heard something about a Thanksgiving dance. One of the guys got invited by a sorority member or something. You inviting me?"

"Well, sort of. I'm inviting Brett, but I thought it might be fun to double-date. You know, like with you and Elissa. The four of us had such a good time at the table in the cafeteria."

Did I really say *that?* I mean what kind of good time can you have in a cafeteria? But it was tough trying to bring up Elissa's name and be subtle about it.

"The four of us, huh?"

He was thinking about it. He hadn't turned me down flat.

He asked, "Does Elissa think it would be fun?"

"Yes. Definitely yes."

"She said so? How come she isn't calling me herself?"

"She can't. I mean I'm the sorority member and as I mentioned, we can't go public yet. But I know she'll go for this idea. The dance is a girls-invite-boys affair at the Palm Canyon Country Club, but it's fine if the boys invite the girls."

"You're saying I should invite Elissa?"

"Well, to go with Brett and me."

"You said the country club? I'd be paying? That could bankrupt me."

I hadn't thought of that. My parents were financing me, but that wouldn't help Eric.

Eric laughed. "I go bankrupt every week. My folks bail me out."

"Does that mean you can go?"

"I *can* go. The question is, *will* I go? What if Elissa doesn't want to go with me?"

I couldn't believe it. He didn't know what I knew. That Elissa had a big crush, or more, on him. Eric wasn't a hunk like Brett. He could use some encouragement.

"She'll go, I guarantee it," I said.

"Guarantees, I don't believe in them. But I'll give it a try. If this is so hush-hush, when do I ask her?"

"Now is fine. But I wouldn't mention *me* right now. Wait until later. Then you can bring up the double-dating."

"This is some mysterious plan you've got here. Did Elissa put you up to it?"

I think he wanted me to answer yes.

"Now what makes you say *that?*" I said.

I'd better watch my step. I wanted to boost his ego, give him a little push. But this plan was mine alone. Encouragement is okay, but manipulation is something else. Eric wanted to go out with Elissa. I had found that out for Elissa. Something she wasn't able to do for herself. He wasn't *dying* to go out with her. Romeo and Juliet this wasn't. I mean, if he absolutely yearned for her he could have asked her himself a long time ago. But this was a start. I figured that by Thanksgiving, Elissa's anger toward me might fade, I'd reveal my matchmaking, and we'd reconcile. Something like that.

Eric was silent.

"Eric?"

"Yup, I'm still Eric. Believe me it's true. It's not a rumor."

I didn't want to kid about his name anymore. I wanted to know his answer.

"Well, are you going to do it?"

"Why not? Life is too short to say no when you can say yes."

"I agree. Call me back and let me know what Elissa says."

"You think she might turn me down?" He sounded hesitant. What if he changed his mind?

"She'll say yes. I'd just like to know what she says."

"If you know she'll say yes, why do you want to know what she says? Never mind. I'll call you back, but I won't tell you anything personal. I don't carry tales or anything."

He was kind of a nice guy. I was glad.

"I have to make another call, Eric. So if my line is busy when you call back, keep trying."

"Will do. So long for now."

"Bye."

I hung up. I had to call Brett. Right now. No waiting until Saturday night. Not with Eric and Elissa falling into place. What a Thanksgiving this was going to be for me! I had taken care of everything. Even Sidney, the boy who was in love with me. The boy who was going to play chess with my father on Thanksgiving weekend. Face it, Sidney wasn't going to go for that. Sidney would be hurt. I'd be all dressed up going out with Brett, possibly in a limo, and Sidney would be hanging around with my folks.

No problem. I could fix that. I could do anything. I was on a roll. Kim Adler, the girl who had once needed a plan to succeed in Palm Canyon, was full of plans. I must have inherited some of my father's creativity.

I telephoned Brett. His father answered. It sounded like his dad anyway, a man's voice. I wished it had been Brett who answered. I was the girl connected to the mutilation of the family car, and Brett's father was still looking for a job. How did he get around without a car? And how did Brett's mother commute to her good job? They needed two cars in the first place and now they had none. I decided not to identify myself.

"May I speak to Brett, please."

"Sure. Hang on."

"Hello."

Brett must have been right by the phone.

"Hi, Brett. It's me, Kim."

"Kim! Hi. What's up?"

"A lot. But first, you've got a sister who's a freshman. That's what you told me, right?"

"That's right."

"I guess she doesn't know many boys yet, being new in town and all of that."

"I don't know. She doesn't tell her big brother much."

"Do you think she'd be interested in meeting a very bright and cute guy from New York, going out with him to a big dance?"

"You want me to ask her? She's right here."

"Okay."

This was great! Sidney could go to the Thanksgiving dance with Brett's sister. We could triple-date with Elissa and Eric. At least Sidney wouldn't be left at home while I swept out of the house in my gown with Brett. I'd get Sidney taken care of now, and I could invite Brett.

"She says to tell her more." Brett was back to the phone.

"Well, I hate to say this because it sounds so

. . . well I don't know what. But anyway, Sidney's extremely rich. He'd probably buy her an orchid or ten orchids for her gown."

"Hold on."

I heard Brett say, "He's rich."

He was back. "She says money is boring. She wants to know about important things."

"Sidney is a kind person."

"Hold on."

I heard Brett say, "Kind person."

He was back. "She says that's better. I think she's sold on the idea. Anything else?"

"Oh, great! No, nothing else. But tell your sister that she'll be dating the most wonderful thirteen-year-old guy in the entire country."

Brett was chuckling. "Hold on."

This time he wasn't back to the phone right away. I waited.

Finally: "Nothing doing. She says thirteen is kindergarten stuff. Nobody under fifteen. Absolute minimum age."

"What? How old is your sister?"

"Thirteen. What's this all about, anyway?"

"Well . . . here it is. I got invited into Chi Kappa Sorority. Actually I became a member last night. You hadn't heard?"

"No, but that's terrific. I guess. Is that what you wanted?"

"Time will tell."

"What's this got to do with my sister and the thirteen-year-old?"

"There's a dance . . . never mind . . . I'll tell you Saturday night, okay? I have a small conflict to work out."

"Well, sure."

"Bye for now."

Eric called me the minute I hung up.

"Elissa didn't understand why I was inviting her to a sorority dance. She said she might go with me and she might not, but how come I didn't ask her out to something plain and normal first. So I did and she said yes. We're going to the movies this Friday."

"Fine," I said. I had lost my enthusiasm for my plans. "You don't happen to have a kid sister, do you, say around nine or ten years old?"

"Not when I last looked."

19

My father was getting busier and busier with his work. He must have missed the fast pace of New York because he agreed to take on an assignment from his old agency. But I had to talk to him. Really talk. About Sidney and chess and what kind of exciting evening Dad might offer Sidney as a consolation prize for my kicking Sidney in the shins by walking out on him. But Dad was getting hard to pin down.

That night after supper, he handed scripts to Mom and me. "Claudine, you're Mrs. Jones. Kim, you're Mr. Jones. I'm the announcer. We're comparing bleaches, Product A and Product B. Claudine, you've just used Product B on your laundry. Go!"

Mom read from her script. "Product B is better!" she yelled.

"Great," Dad said. "Now you scream at the top of your lungs, keel over, and suffer a heart attack from the shock of Product B being better."

"Why?"

"No questions. I'm smiling into the camera. I say, 'Mrs. Jones was quite surprised to discover that Product B, Blitz! bleach, *does* in fact whiten better than Product A.' Now there are sirens in the background, and we see paramedics coming in with a lot of fancy equipment. They try to revive you. They start screaming for more equipment as Mr. Jones—that's you, Kim—walks in looking rather distressed."

"Dad, I am distressed. Can I talk to you about something?"

"In a minute. You're supposed to look at the paramedics working over your wife and ask, 'What happened to my wife?' Then I say, 'Well, Mr. Jones, your wife has just discovered that new Blitz! bleach with SmashAction whitens better than the other leading brand.' Go on, Kim."

I read, "Oh really? That surprises me too. But now that I'm the one who's going to have to do all the bleaching in the family I'll be sure to try Blitz! because I've seen with my own eyes that Blitz! is really better."

Mom spoke up. "I'm on the floor, Harris. Breathing hard. Okay? Now I'm gasping my last words: 'I'm just *amazed!*' "

"Great!" Dad said. "They put a sheet over you and carry you out while you, Kim, pretend you're holding up a white towel, and smile as your kids join you. Meanwhile I'm holding up a box of Blitz! 'Blitz! *does* work better!' I say."

"Dad," I said. "Don't people take bleach seriously? I mean, can you get away with this?"

"It's one approach. We'll see. I was asked for fresh ideas, and this is one of them."

"Can I get up now?" Mom asked.

"Can I talk to you, Dad?" I asked.

"Questions, questions. No to the first, yes to the second."

"Very funny," Mom said, brushing herself off. "I should have vacuumed first."

"Sit by the pool?" Dad asked me.

"Sure. Want to join us, Mom? This isn't really private."

"No, I'll just clean up a bit in the kitchen, and hope that I don't faint if the results are too good."

The evening air felt nice. "Dad," I asked as soon as we sat down, "is Sidney crazy about chess? How do you think he'd feel about spending an evening playing chess with you while I go to a dance with another guy?"

"How do *you* think he'd feel, Kim?"

That was my answer, pure and simple.

"I was planning to ask Brett to the Thanksgiving dance the sorority is having."

"Oh, the one that's going to cost me a mint? Your mother told me."

"They're giving some of the money to charity."

"That sounds worthwhile."

"It sounds better than it is."

I wasn't supposed to talk about the sorority's finances. But that ten percent had been nagging me. I told my father as much as I knew. He hesitated while he did some figuring in his head. Finally he said, "I'd estimate that your sorority is going to raise exactly one bowl of soup for that tribe in South America."

"I don't understand why they can't give all the profits to charity. Most of the girls are well off, if not rich."

"Simple, Kim. First the sorority wants to stay financially afloat on its own terms. They'll never have enough money, according to their own definition of money. They'll never have enough power according to their own definition of power. They'll never have enough of anything."

My father was edging very close to one of his talks on morality, capitalism, conscience, and of course, groups. I already had the general idea. I knew he didn't like the sorority. I'd be surprised if he paid for a limo for the dance. A limo? The dance? Was I going? Yes, I was going.

With Sidney Megovitch.

20

Brett's car wasn't fixed by Saturday night. We took a bus to a movie. I got my first kiss from him on the bus. I got more at my front door afterwards. I waited until we were there before I told him about my situation. I waited until after my kisses.

"The sorority is having a dance Thanksgiving weekend. Girls invite boys. That's the dance I wanted to fix your sister up with my friend for. I'm not saying that right, am I?"

"You're doing fine. But I'll help you. I say yes."

"Yes to what?"

"Yes, I'll go with you."

"Oh, no!"

"Thanks for the enthusiasm." He was laughing.

He thought I was kidding.

"I *want* to go with you, Brett. Believe me."

"Okay, I do. Sounds like there's more coming. What's the problem?"

"The problem—although I hate to call him that—is my thirteen-year-old friend, the one I wanted your sister to go out with. He invited himself to my house for Thanksgiving—all the way from New York—and . . ."

"All the way from New York? He must like you."

"He *loves* me. He wants to marry me. See, that's the problem, about hurting him and . . ."

"He wants to *marry* you? He's the one who's rich and cute—and I believe you said kind also?"

"Are you making fun of him?"

"No, but I don't quite get it."

"You don't get why someone would want to marry me?"

"I didn't say that."

Was Brett making fun of Sidney? Nobody could make fun of my friend Sidney and get away with it!

"Sidney's great," I said.

"You like him better than me?"

"He's just a friend."

"A friend who wants to marry you?"

"Let's forget that part. I tried to fix him up with your sister so I could go to the dance with *you*. Get it?"

"I get it. But you're going with Sidney?"

"I have to. I mean if I go at all. And all the sorority girls are expected to go."

"Okay, okay. I see that you're in a tight spot."

"I'm sorry."

"It's okay. I'll call you again when my car's fixed."

"I like buses too."

21

It was time for another sorority meeting. I crammed for an exam all day so that I could go to the meeting at night. Not that I was looking forward to watching Crystal Jameson get sworn in. But I didn't feel as nervous as the last time. I knew what to expect. And I wouldn't be their *newest* member.

I was feeling pretty calm about everything now. I had made peace with my situation. I knew I'd be going to the Thanksgiving dance with Sidney. I hoped he had grown since the last time I saw him, but I wasn't counting on it. There's a sprouting-up period for teenagers, which in Sidney's case would probably begin the moment he left Palm Canyon.

Elissa still wasn't speaking to me, but I saw her and Eric together at school a couple of times, and that made me feel good. Brett was friendly to me but he said he wanted to wait until he got his car back before going out again. At least that's the excuse he gave me. I hoped he was jealous of Sidney instead of being angry at me.

I took a break from my studying and went into the kitchen for something to eat. Dinner was a few hours away, and lunch had been an unsuccessful try by my father at making bean and cheese burritos for the three of us. Now Dad was in the kitchen stuffing himself on a New York deli-type sandwich. "I know who I am, what my limitations are, and the basic cosmic plan for my stomach," he explained as he pointed to his pastrami on rye with mustard and pickle. "Want me to make you one?"

"A sandwich or a cosmic plan?"

"One of each coming up," he said. He took a bite out of his sandwich. "But first you have to pay for it. Tell me what you think of a ghost family bragging about their bleach? What's whiter than ghosts? Now if they used Blitz! bleach . . ."

The telephone rang.

"It's the ghost family," I said, "wanting to know how much they'll get paid for appearing in your commercial. They want enough money so that if they die, their children will be taken care of."

My father answered the phone. Then he motioned to me and held out the receiver. He was shrugging his shoulders as if to say he didn't know who was calling. But he whispered in my ear, "Her voice is slippery slick. Like the skin on an uncooked fish."

I nudged my father and took the receiver. I said hello. I refrained from adding "Fish voice."

"Hi," the voice said. Then it paused.

Who was it? I waited. Was the voice going to pause forever? Some kids use pauses very effectively. Like, suspense time, what comes next? The telephone company must love the pause people when they get on long-distance.

"This is Crystal Jameson." At last the pause ended. But why was Crystal Jameson calling *me?* What did she want? She had to want something.

"Yes, Crystal."

"I'm getting sworn in tonight at the sorority meeting."

"I know."

"Well, I thought it might be fun if we went together. The two newest members."

The voice became soft and shy. Velvet fishskin. Was this an obscene phone call? There was no profanity, no dirty words, nothing indecent or disgusting. That was the trouble with it. It was too *nice.*

Now it was my turn to pause. I didn't want to go to the meeting with her. I needed a quick excuse.

She said, "We're going to be sorority sisters!"

This was positively an obscene phone call. I had to report it to the telephone company. *Sorority sisters!* It sounded so close, so intimate, and so revolting.

I said, "I don't drive and you don't drive so what did you have in mind?"

"My dad can take us."

The midget? I kept myself from saying it. I could find out if he was, or on the other hand, could qualify for gianthood, as advertised.

"That's not very convenient for him . . ."

She knew I was trying to get out of it. She switched subjects abruptly. "Are you going to the sorority's Thanksgiving dance?"

"My plans aren't finalized." The less I said, the better.

"Who are you taking?" She kept on going.

"Look, you've got a few hours before you become a member. You're not there yet. I'm not free to discuss sorority business with you at this time."

I could fool around with the English language and stuffy phrases and any kind of word games I wanted, but it all came down to one thing: she was going to invite Brett but she wanted to make sure I hadn't already done it. And the way I was sparring around with her gave her hope. People who have to choreograph their conversations—five words forward, seven words backward—are in trouble. And I started to do it. "Crystal, I can say that . . . no I can't say right now that . . . that is . . . Crystal, good-bye!"

I decided to skip the sorority meeting.

22

Sidney Megovitch hadn't grown an inch. Not to the north or the east or the west. He wasn't taller or broader or fuller or older. Please, a little older. But no. Time had stood still for Sidney Megovitch. My parents and I met him at the airport. He had come in on a regional airline out of Phoenix. And of course he came bearing gifts. Sidney always gave the kind of gifts you'd expect from a seasoned, sophisticated grown-up who had been around the world a dozen times and knew what the best years for wines were, country by country. Mom got imported crystal, Dad got a genuine leather imported briefcase, and I got a ring that looked suspiciously, dangerously like a diamond. Were we engaged?

We all told Sidney he shouldn't have done it. I really meant it. Sidney wouldn't give me a *glass* ring. Unless I was lucky. I'd have to discuss this with Mom or Dad after he left. Or before he left. But right now he was settling into his guest suite downstairs, after making us unwrap our gifts first.

He looked so cute and so small. Why did he have to be small for his age? Perhaps the Arizona climate might cause him to sprout, I told myself.

I helped him hang up his things. He grabbed me and gave me a long, sexy kiss. Right then and there I knew the ring was a diamond.

"You're a wonderful friend, Sidney," I said.

"Friend?" he said. "What a sterile word. Put my ring on."

"About your ring, is it a . . . a . . . what's it made of?"

"It's nothing. It's just a beginner diamond. Like training wheels or something. It should fit your little fingers. I had it made up that way."

I put the ring on my little right finger. It fit.

"There you are," he said. And there I was.

Sidney grew a little during our Thanksgiving dinner. He ate a lot and stuffed his stomach. After dinner we showed Sidney around town. He stroked my hand whenever possible. It occurred to me that if any other guy came on to me as strong as Sidney did, I'd give him a shove that would land him in California. Cutesie puppies can get away with anything. Adopt me, adopt me!

My parents had decided to pay for a limo to take Sidney and me to the sorority dance. They also paid for the most beautiful dress I'd ever seen. Sidney of course had a tux. He looked . . . adoptable.

I felt so nervous when the limo arrived at the front of our house. Sidney was used to limos. Mom and Dad practically pushed us out the door. It was suddenly all too much for me, going to the dance with Sidney instead of Brett. I knew Crystal would be there with Brett. She had made sure that I knew they were going together. Brett never mentioned it. We had gone out a couple of times after I broke the news to him about Sidney. I knew Brett liked me, but not enough to say no to Crystal I guess. Or maybe he didn't believe that Sidney was just a friend.

It was glamorous, I mean really glamorous, being whisked off in that limo. Sidney tipped the driver one hundred dollars when we got to the Palm Canyon Country Club.

The country club was gorgeous. I had seen it once in the daytime. Now it was full of lights and I could hear music coming from the main building and see people streaming in. In back of all of this, the mountains rose majestically, as mountains do.

Sidney and I walked into the room where the dance was being held. I nodded to a couple I recognized who entered the same time we did. I was glad Sidney and I weren't making a solo entrance. I wasn't really embarrassed at being seen with juvenile Sidney. I was proud to have a devoted friend like him. He had come all the way from New York, hadn't he? I had made sure that I spread that piece of information around school in advance of the dance. It was an act of vanity—or an act of apology for Sidney's shockingly youthful appearance. I hoped it was an act of vanity.

I saw Crystal and Brett first thing. I was glad. It was better than preparing myself for the sight of them together, and thinking that any minute I'd run into them. I expected Crystal to be clinging to Brett, but she was too cool to cling. They were talking to another couple. Crystal was wearing a smashing gown which unfortunately looked fantastic on her. Brett was dressed in a kind of tux. It was different from Sidney's. Because of the wonderful room and the clothes and the music and all that, Brett and Crystal looked as if they belonged together. All the dates I had had with him seemed so minor, as if a dozen of them would never add up to the importance of being with him tonight. This affair looked like a celebration for the winner, and the winner was Crystal.

Sidney said that I looked very New York and that I should never forget my New York heritage. I wondered if anyone noticed the diamond sparkling on my little finger.

Some of the couples were dancing, some were standing around the buffet tables, and some were just standing around. I picked out the sorority girls. All present and accounted for. A few of the girls were going steady and they of course invited their boyfriends. Selena, Allie, and Tracy had imported their guys from out of town. Phoenix I think. Or Tucson.

The room was filling up. There were, by Allie's computation at the last meeting, over fifty couples who had purchased tickets. There would be money left over for her charity. But only ten percent of the profit. It still didn't sit right with me that this had been promoted as a charity dance, over Tracy's objections, over my objections. I remembered what my father had said about how little the charity would benefit from all of this. One bowl of soup. He was being more symbolic than accurate, but he probably wasn't far off the mark.

"Want to dance?"

Sidney held out his arm. I had already pictured myself towering over him on the dance floor. I had towered over him numerous times in my mind before the dance. I knew that would be the hardest part of Sidney to accept.

"This is wonderful," he said as he stepped on my foot. I hadn't anticipated that.

"Having a good time, Sidney?"

"Super. The Thanksgiving dinner was super, this weekend is super, and you're super. Marry me, Kim."

"We'll talk about it in a few years, Sidney, okay?"

"Yes, I've accepted that. I'll come visit you in the meantime. Palm Canyon blows me away. I'll bring Shannon."

"Okay."

It was getting to be a sweet kind of evening. Sidney was loving it. He swung me around the floor with an enthusiastic jerkiness, a hallmark of being thirteen. We almost bumped into Elissa and Eric. There they were, a couple, thanks to me, but no thanks to me because Elissa ignored me and probably didn't know I had brought her and Eric together. I didn't care if she knew. I just wanted us to be friends again.

Sidney was gaining speed and confidence on the dance floor. We collided with Brett and Crystal. I could have sworn that Sidney did it on purpose, but how could he know about Brett and me? My father wouldn't have said anything, would he?

"Sorry." Sidney looked at Brett and Crystal with mock apology.

Crystal said, "Who are you?" to Sidney.

"Sidney Megovitch of New York City. Who are you?"

"Crystal Jameson, and this is my date, Brett Fox."

I knew that at some point in the evening Crystal would make sure that she paraded Brett in front of me. She had decided to take advantage of this collision with Sidney and me. Her pretended interest in Sidney was transparent. Brett was staring at Sidney. Next to Sidney, Brett looked taller than usual, and next to Brett, Sidney looked shorter than usual. Didn't Brett realize that Sidney was just my young friend, my pal? Brett smiled at me, but that could mean nothing.

Crystal asked Sidney, "Is this your first formal dance?"

A barb.

"It's my first one in a hick town," Sidney replied.

Sidney could take care of himself.

"Care to dance?" Brett asked me.

Crystal's eyes narrowed.

"I'd love it," I said.

"Crystal baby?" Sidney said mockingly, extending his arm toward Crystal.

"You look beautiful," Brett said as we moved away together.

"Careful. Crystal might hear you."

"Here's hoping."

Did he mean it? He wasn't angry, that's for sure.

"Why did you accept Crystal? Why did you come with her?"

"You came with somebody. It's only a dance. It's not forever. It's . . ."

Brett didn't get a chance to finish his sentence. The dance music stopped abruptly and the band played a few notes with a flourish, like making an announcement. Allie Grendler had walked up on the musicians' stage and grabbed a mike.

Crystal meanwhile had grabbed Brett away from me. Our dance was over, we were over, as far as she was concerned.

Allie spoke into the mike. "Greetings," she said cheerfully. "And a little quiet, please."

"What for, Allie?" someone yelled good-naturedly.

"An announcement," she said. "I'm happy to say that Chi Kappa Sorority has tonight raised a hefty sum for charity thanks to all of you enthusiastic folks out there who came to our Thanksgiving bash."

Some of the sorority girls led the applause. But I didn't join in. Hefty sum? I don't clap for one bowl of soup.

The applause finally stopped. Then Elissa's

voice, loud and clear, rang out. "How hefty, Allie?"

A few kids laughed as if this was just friendly heckling coming from Elissa.

Allie laughed too.

But Elissa asked again, "How hefty, Allie?"

Allie stopped laughing. The room was quiet. "Elissa," Allie said, "you're not a member of the sorority. We don't discuss our finances with *outsiders.*"

Outsiders! What a cruel thing to say in front of everybody. I could see Allie gliding through life, dropping her verbal litter everywhere.

Everyone was looking at Elissa. Eric patted her arm. It was a gesture of support. But what could he really do?

"How hefty, Allie?"

This time it wasn't Elissa asking. It was me! I didn't wait for an answer. I said, *"I'm* a member of the sorority and I'm asking. *How hefty, Allie?"*

The room erupted. Underneath all the formal clothes, the gowns, the tuxes, the corsages, the silver and gold slippers, the jewelry, the whole glamorous spread, these were high school kids. These were the kids who cheered and heckled and whistled at football games and tennis matches and sometimes in assembly. These were the kids who threw things in the cafeteria. And now they had a catch-phrase that caught their spirit: "HOW HEFTY, ALLIE? HOW HEFTY, ALLIE?"

With a fixed smile on her face, Allie Grendler stormed off the stage. She walked up to me. "How dare you!" she said.

The room went quiet again.

"I dare," I said. "I dare. I *quit* Chi Kappa Sorority!"

I was shaking. Why did I do it? Was it the charity thing or the fat Elissa thing or Buckingham Palace or what? It didn't matter. It would have happened eventually.

I felt so conspicuous. Sidney took my hand. He would never stop loving me now.

He said to me, "A bowl of soup."

My father must have told him.

Sidney pulled his wallet out of his pocket. "This dance is going to raise money for charity whether the sorority likes it or not!" he shouted.

Then he pulled out a bunch of one-hundred-dollar bills and tossed them into the air. "One thousand dollars for charity!" he shouted.

Sidney looked taller than Brett. He looked taller than anybody. Sidney had become a hero.

Kids like heroes. Especially improbable

ones whom they don't find threatening. Sidney filled the bill. The kids actually cheered.

Brett moved away from Crystal toward me. But Crystal pulled him back. That was the only way she could have him now. By pulling. But let Brett worry about me a little, fight over me if necessary.

This was a triumphant moment for me, but triumphant moments don't last. Only their consequences. What would happen to me now? Would I be snubbed, loved, hated, admired . . . what? I would be talked about and whispered about. I had quit the sorority. I didn't belong anymore. I didn't agree with my father that all groups are bad. I had liked being part of a group. There was a place in my life for it. I could, if I wanted to, start my own group, my own sorority. It would be hard to buck the entrenched sorority. But it could be done.

I saw Elissa looking at me. So what? Everyone was looking at Sidney and me. But then Elissa rushed toward me in a wonderful ballet of eager, awkward steps. Elissa, my friend.

About the Author

MARJORIE SHARMAT is one of the most popular and prolific authors of best-selling books for today's young readers. Her more than eighty books, published in thirteen languages, have sold over twelve million copies. Among her novels for young adults are *Square Pegs, I Saw Him First, How To Meet A Gorgeous Guy, How To Meet A Gorgeous Girl,* and *How To Have A Gorgeous Wedding,* all available in Laurel-Leaf editions. Her most recent novels include *He Noticed I'm Alive . . . and Other Hopeful Signs* and its companion volume, *Two Guys Noticed Me . . . and Other Miracles.* Ms. Sharmat lives in Tucson, Arizona.

Meet Glenwood High's fabulous four, the

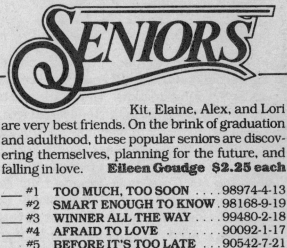

Kit, Elaine, Alex, and Lori are very best friends. On the brink of graduation and adulthood, these popular seniors are discovering themselves, planning for the future, and falling in love. **Eileen Goudge $2.25 each**

___ #1	TOO MUCH, TOO SOON	98974-4-13
___ #2	SMART ENOUGH TO KNOW	98168-9-19
___ #3	WINNER ALL THE WAY	99480-2-18
___ #4	AFRAID TO LOVE	90092-1-17
___ #5	BEFORE IT'S TOO LATE	90542-7-21
___ #6	TOO HOT TO HANDLE	98812-8-27
___ #7	HANDS OFF, HE'S MINE	93359-3-27
___ #8	FORBIDDEN KISSES	92674-2-19
___ #9	A TOUCH OF GINGER	98816-0-15
___ #10	PRESENTING SUPERHUNK	97172-1-23
___ #11	BAD GIRL	90467-6-22
___ #12	DON'T SAY GOODBYE	92108-2-31
___ #13	KISS AND MAKE UP	94514-3-19